INJURED HEROES SERIES - BOOK THREE

CROSSROADS OF
REDEMPTION

DANIELLE M HAAS

To my sister, Caitlin. Thank you for always being by my side when I need a shoulder to cry on, a kick in the pants, or a friend to laugh with. My life is so much sweeter with you in it.

1

The sun crawled above the peaks of the Smoky Mountains, its warm beams a welcome sight as Mia Tulley picked her way through the too-high grass. Dew still clung to the vibrant green blades, the moisture wicking against the thin material of her black leggings. But she didn't mind. Rain had poured down on Pine Valley, Tennessee for the past five days. But today's promise of clear skies had her yearning to stretch her legs along the wooded paths and inhale the fresh, springtime air.

Had her yearning to be far away from the duplex she rented, not realizing she'd share a wall with the brooding pain in her backside she was forced to work with at Crossroads Mountain Retreat—a rehabilitation center tucked away in the mountains for injured law enforcement officers and veterans.

Chet Black was unlike any man she'd ever met and thank God for that. If his size wasn't intimidating enough, add in the surly attitude and constant frown buried beneath his thick beard, and he was downright terrifying. But she wouldn't let him scare her off. Not when she desperately needed a new beginning away from the prying eyes of her hometown in the next county over.

No, Pine Valley offered her everything she needed to heal—to grow from the shocking betrayal that had cut her at her knees, leaving her with nothing. And if she had to make nice with the chef at the retreat while she climbed back up on her own two feet, so be it. She hadn't moved here to make friends. She moved here to lick her wounds and come out of her living nightmare a better person.

If she could do that by enjoying the amazing view of the mountains from the tiny porch of her new apartment, even better. She'd just continue to ignore the man who lived— and worked—beside her. Letting another man get her down wouldn't happen again in this lifetime. Chet Black would just have to put up with her until it was time to move on to bigger and better things.

The sound of squeaking hinges echoed around her. Feeling the heat of Chet's gaze on her back, she rolled her eyes. She wouldn't give him the satisfaction of turning with a good morning wave, not like he'd appreciate the gesture anyway. If she had it her way, she'd gladly give him a different gesture with her right hand, but that wouldn't be nice. And damnit it all to hell, the stupid manners her mama had ingrained in her since birth weren't something she could just forget.

Even though being too nice—and a little bit naïve—was what had landed her in her current predicament.

Gritting her teeth, she pushed all thoughts of her crumbling life and ungrateful ex and jerk neighbor from her mind and hopped over a fallen log to get on a trail that led through the woods. She'd arrived in Pine Valley in the winter, so she hadn't explored many paths that surrounded the cute cabin-turned-duplex she'd found tucked deep within the forest. Then came the rain. So much rain.

But now the sun was out, and she was on a mission to discover her new home. Mud caked onto the bottom of her boots, making her steps more difficult than normal. A backpack sat heavy on her shoulders. She didn't plan to be gone long but being prepared was another one of those lessons ingrained in her. Better to not be caught unaware and all that.

A lesson that struck a little close to home of late—one she'd failed to remember.

Mia might have let love blind her and leave her unprepared for her new future, but that wouldn't be the case for today's hike. A quick half-mile walk to a picture-perfect spot to watch the sun finish its climb above the mountains before heading to the retreat to start her day's work. Hopefully she'd find enough zen in her time with nature to keep her level headed for a day stuck in the kitchen with Chet.

The wide trail narrowed, and the incline steepened. A deep ravine stretched along the valley floor to her side. Dead foliage rustled at her feet. Mia grunted as she watched her footing on the slick terrain. Sweat dotted her hairline, and she wiped it off with the back of her wrist, pushing aside her pesky black curls that refused to stay secured in her stubby ponytail. A fascinating mixture of majestic maples and towering oaks surrounded her, their budding leaves exploding above her like fireworks, only allowing glimpses of the clear blue sky along the edges of the green shapes.

Shafts of light beckoned her forward, and she quickened her pace up the hill. Her calve muscles screamed in protest. The mud on her boots hardened, making the moist path more difficult to navigate. Her feet slid out from under her, and a squeak of panic echoed off the thick tree trunks. Her arm shot out, and she latched onto a nearby branch to steady herself.

The thin twig snapped free and threw off her precarious balance. Her body shifted to the side, her momentum toppling her to the ground. She landed with a hard thud on a slick pile of leaves and slid down the ravine. She clawed at the grass and stones tumbling down the hill alongside her. Water seeped through the material of her pants. She dug her heels into the ground, her forward trajectory coming to a grinding halt.

She lifted dirt-covered hands and grimaced. Well darn. So much for a quick walk then off to work. She'd definitely have to shower and change before going anywhere. Tiny pricks of pain on the backs of her thighs made her cringe. Standing, she swiped her dirty palms against her pants and hoisted the still intact pack on her shoulders. She turned to head up the hill to get back on the trail toward home and something poking out from the newly upturned ground caught her eye.

Something long and thin, the color of tanned skin.

A lump of fear lodged in her throat, but she tiptoed toward the long stretch of shallow tunnel her heels had dug in the earth. She peered down and gasped. A finger pointed upward, reaching toward the sky like Michelangelo's painting. Covering her mouth with her hands, she backpedaled before tripping over an exposed root and landing on her back side.

With eyes latched onto the exposed hand, she screamed.

CHET BLACK LEANED against the back of the red rocking chair on the porch he was now forced to share with that damn woman. The woman who'd barged into *his* kitchen, buzzing around like an annoying gnat. Always in the way. Always around.

He could pop Bobby's scrawny neck like a pimple for renting the other half of the duplex to Mia without first asking him. Solitude was what Chet sought more than anything—the only reason he'd chosen to rent the small apartment from the local handyman. A tucked away cabin Bobby had converted into two apartments, renting the property to aid his retirement.

Now Chet was never alone. The thin wall that separated him from Mia didn't do much to mute the constant noise that surrounded her like a cloud of dust that kid from the Peanuts cartoon was always consumed under. Banging around, doing God knew what, disturbing his peace and grating against his nerves.

Not like he was ever really at peace. Not since his wife and daughter had been brutally ripped away from him— right in front of his eyes.

The thick skin ringing his wrists burned, as though his flesh would melt against his bones. The steaming cup of coffee in his hand hindered him from rubbing the old wounds—the constant reminders of a past he'd never unsee. Never forget. The images of his family in their last moments on earth forever burned into his brain just like the sick symbol singed into his forearm.

Grinding his teeth, he focused on evening his breathing with his gaze set on the rising sun. He let the blinding glare of the bright rays sting his retinas. He focused on the pain. On the harsh sensation that brought tears to his eyes—tears that for once, weren't a reaction to living without the two people he loved most. His heart outside his body that had been broken and battered then buried in graves he refused to visit. Because Laurie and Riley weren't in the cold ground. Hell, they weren't anywhere. He was all by himself, left to move on when taking one damn breath was sometimes the hardest thing he ever had to do.

Well, at least he *was* alone. Until Mia Tulley burst into his kitchen at Crossroads Mountain Retreat and turned his already messed-up life upside down. He still hadn't forgiven Brooke—his boss and owner of the retreat—for insisting he needed an assistant. He'd gotten along just fine without help. He didn't need some pixie of a woman with the raven black curls and annoyingly positive attitude stepping on his toes.

He definitely didn't need her invading his thoughts at night when he curled under the comforter he'd shared with his wife.

Taking a sip of bitter, black coffee, he snuck a peek at his watch. Almost time to leave for work. Fatigue made climbing to his feet harder than it should be. He stretched a hand above his head then turned for the door.

A high-pitched scream erupted through the trees and squeezed his chest. Setting his coffee down on the thick wooden railing surrounding the porch, he jogged down the stairs and followed the deep impressions Mia's boots had left in the mud. He quickened his pace then swore under his breath when he realized the path Mia had taken for her morning hike.

He should have spoken up when he'd watched her leave the apartment this morning. The terrain on this side of the forest would be soggy after all the rain they'd gotten lately, which could be dangerous for someone who wasn't familiar with the trail.

Hell, he'd barely been on these trails. He preferred to sit on the porch or stick to the back of the house, fishing in the small pond that nestled close to his home. The steep incline and rocky edges of the cliff face were a challenge he seldom took on.

"Mia!" He called out her name, hoping a snake had slithered across the path or something equally ridiculous had spooked her. He stepped carefully as he climbed over loose stones and wet mud sucked his booted foot to the earth.

"Over here," her shaky voice called out.

He stopped, craning his neck to the side to search for her. He'd assumed she'd be further up the mountain, but her voice didn't sound too far away. An arm waved high, the flash of a bright red sleeve drawing his attention. He weaved through the trees, relieved that Mia didn't appear injured and irritated by her hysterics. Screeching in the woods like a banshee for no good reason wasn't something he'd tolerate, and he had no trouble telling her that.

Mia lowered her hand then crossed her arms over her stomach, her gaze glued to something on the ground. A paleness had transformed her dark skin, and her teeth clattered against each other.

Chet picked his way to her side, concern clouding over his annoyance. "Mia? What's wrong?"

Without looking at him, she pointed toward the ground.

He followed the long line of her finger and dread settled into the pit of his stomach. What the hell? What looked like a hand, finger extended back at Mia, poked up from the newly upturned earth.

"I...I fell," Mia said, her words coming out on spurts of stuttered breath. "My heels dragged through the mud when I tried to stop, and when I stood, I noticed the finger." She swallowed hard then pressed a fist against her sealed lips.

His mouth went dry. He might have been off the police force for the past three years, but his training kicked in. Not wanting to touch anything, but needing to know what in the world he was looking at, Chet stepped slowly toward the limb. The hand was bloated and stiff, and the hint of decay in the wind told him whoever the hand belonged to hadn't been dead for too long. Keeping his distance, he crouched low and noticed the unsettled dirt around the forearm, indicating the rest of the body was hidden beneath the ground. He needed to call the police and get officers out here immediately. Standing, he dug his phone from the front pocket of his jeans. A mark on the inside of the wrist made his heart stop. He leaned forward, squinting to make out the shape that marred the smooth skin.

A raised symbol stared back at him, the delicate swoops that turned the light skin red making bile burn his stomach lining. Lifting the sleeve of his flannel shirt, he grazed the pad of his thumb over the same symbol, the angry red long gone, replaced by a bright white scar he would never be rid of.

The scar his wife and daughter's killer had branded him with before leaving him in a burning house to die.

And now the asshole was back. But this time, Chet would find him, and when he did, he'd make him pay for taking away his entire world—and leaving him alive to deal with the pain.

2

Mia sat hunched over on a wide stump, the fallen tree laid out behind her. Her stomach churned, and she kept her eyes squeezed shut, not wanting to bear witness to the chaos around her. Not wanting to see the poor woman who still laid in the ground, the top layer of earth now uncovered to show her broken body. No matter where Mia's life took her, she'd never erase the image of the blue-tinged lips and waxen skin from her memory.

She should have hurried back to her apartment after she'd given her statement to Officer Lincoln Sawyer, but she hadn't wanted to return alone. And no amount of insistence from Officer Sawyer could persuade Chet to leave the crime scene.

A gentle hand on her shoulder had Mia opening her eyes and casting her gaze upward. Brooke Mather stood in front of her, concern snapping her brows low. "How are you holding up?"

Mia let out a long breath before pushing to her feet. A chill danced up her arms despite the warm weather. "Not good. I can't believe I uncovered a dead body. Officer Sawyer doesn't think she's been there long. The dirt covering her was so loose—freshly turned over." Fear and sorrow lodged in her throat and made her voice crack. "Who would kill a woman then bury her in the woods? And so close to my home."

Brooke hooked an arm over her shoulder. "Let's get you out of here. There's no reason for you to stand around and watch what has to happen next. Lincoln's got her now," she said, nodding toward the corpse that would forever haunt Mia's dreams.

"What about Chet?" She watched her neighbor, concern coiling her insides. If possible, the big man seemed more upset by the gruesome discovery than her.

"Chet can take care of himself." A sadness echoed through Brooke's words as she scooped Mia's bag from the forest floor and secured it on her back.

Unable to tear her gaze from Chet, Mia twisted her lips. "He looks more troubled than I feel, if that's possible. Leaving him here doesn't seem right."

Brooke gave her a gentle tug, turning her toward the steep hill. "Chet has a lot of demons, and this is bringing some of them back to life. Best to let him deal with them how he sees fit."

Questions burned Mia's tongue, but she swallowed them. Digging into other people's lives wasn't a habit she wanted to start.

Forcing her attention forward, she climbed back up the incline she'd tumbled down. Dried mud caked her pants and hands. A bead of sweat slid down the side of her face. Brooke kept a steady hand on her arm, which she was grateful for. Her body was heavy, each step difficult. Birds chirped from their spots perched in the trees, combining with Mia's ragged pants as she found the even terrain of the trail and sighed. The sound of men chattering about death loomed behind her.

"Do you want some water?" Brooke dug inside the pack she'd grabbed from Mia, fishing out a water bottle.

"Thanks." Mia popped open the top and gulped down the cold water. Her hand shook, causing a river of liquid to run down the corner of her mouth before wiping it away. The commotion at the bottom of the ravine drew her attention like a car crash—she shouldn't look but couldn't stop herself. "How long do you think she was buried down there?"

Brooke shrugged. "I didn't look at the body, and Lincoln didn't mention details when he called."

Blinking, Mia focused on Brooke. Sunlight spilled through the interwoven leaves and showcased the copper highlights in her brown hair. "Why *did* Lincoln call you? Weren't you at work?" Alarm rang through her, and she cringed. "Oh no! Breakfast. Chet and I were both here. We left you short staffed. I'm so sorry."

"Are you serious?" Brooke placed a reassuring palm on Mia's forearm. "What you're experiencing is so traumatic. The last thing you need to worry about is if the breakfast was served on time at the retreat, which by the way, it was." Brooke offered a sweet smile, but concern still clouded her brown eyes. "Lincoln called because he was worried about you and figured you'd want someone with you."

Needing a minute to collect herself, Mia leaned against the hard bark of a towering maple and sank to the ground. "I just keep seeing it. Her hand pointed up at me. Like she was reaching for someone to help her. To save her."

Brooke settled on the ground beside her, legs bent and arms hooked over her knees. "You weren't able to save her, but you found her. Probably long before she would have been found otherwise. Which gives Lincoln and the rest of the police department a better chance of finding the person who did this."

Mia inhaled a deep breath, pulling in the scents of wild-flowers and still-damp grass. But the toxic smell of death refused to go away. "Whoever's responsible is out there. Maybe hurting someone else." Fear grabbed hold of her throat as a thought fought its way through the lingering shock and fog. "What if he saw me?"

Straightening, Brooke studied her with a faint hint of panic edging out the soft planes of her petite face. "Did you see anything unusual? Anyone walking on the trail?"

Mia shook her head. "No. I told Lincoln as much when I gave him my statement." A chill swept through her, and she rubbed her palms over her arms, but it did nothing to stop the sensation that someone was watching her—that she stumbled upon something much bigger than all the bullshit she'd walked away from when Aaron took off and left her with nothing.

At least she had her life. Her health. A plan for the future. Unlike the poor soul left behind to rot alone in the forest. "But what if I missed something? What if someone saw me even if I didn't see them?" The thought had her studying the dense woods. A killer who'd bury a dead body in a shallow grave in a ravine would know how to stay under the radar. Keep hidden and out of sight.

And if she'd walked right into that sightline, she might have just put a big red target on the middle of her back.

THE SCARS on Chet's wrists itched. He circled his palm around one wrist to ease the maddening sensation. Not like it helped. Nothing ever helped.

"You really should head back home." Lincoln rested a heavy hand on his shoulder. Dirt and sweat mixed on his face, the flecks of mud sticking to his beard. "It's been a long ass morning. You should get some rest."

The body of the dead woman was long gone, taken to the morgue by the coroner, but he kept his gaze on the broken earth where she'd rested. She hadn't been there long, possibly mere hours or even minutes before Mia uncovered her resting place. Who had put her there? So many questions built inside him, he just might explode. "It's gotta be him, man. The same sonofabitch who killed my family."

Dropping his hand, Lincoln shrugged. "Could be. Could be something completely unrelated."

Lincoln's casual tone turned Chet's blood to fire. Lincoln was new to Pine Valley, not quite a year spent on the local police force after moving to town from Nashville. He hadn't been around when Chet's life had been destroyed. Hadn't seen the symbol that marred his wife and child's skin, just as it scarred his own.

"No chance in hell that whoever burned that symbol into the poor woman's arm isn't the same person who did this." He shoved up the red and black flannel sleeve and jammed a finger against the marred skin on the inside of his forearm.

Lincoln's face remained passive, but a vein ticked at his temple. "I'm not saying it's not. I'm saying I need to look at the whole picture. I can't jump to conclusions."

Chet took a step forward, pushing into Lincoln's personal space. "You and I both know coincidences are bullshit. The same person who put this woman in the ground took everything from me."

"What if he's not the one who killed her?" Lincoln asked, standing his ground. "What if he burned her but she survived like you? What if someone else finished her off and left her in the cold ground? I know you want to find who took your family from you. Hell, I hardly know you, but I want to find that sonofabitch, too. But I have to do my job. Have to follow all the pieces I find and jam them together until I figure out what happened."

Frustration mounted in Chet's chest, pressure building until it nearly choked him. The sound of a handful of officers scouring the surrounding woods buzzed in his ears. A dull thud pounded against the center of his forehead. Sweat tickled the back of his neck. He rubbed his sternum, moving his palm back and forth—back and forth—but nothing stopped the sense of impending suffocation gripping him.

Lincoln clapped a hand between his shoulder blades, gently pushing him forward until he bent at the waist and rested his forearms on his knees.

"Deep breaths in through the nose," Lincoln said. "Nice and steady."

Chet squeezed his eyes shut and concentrated on filling his lungs with air.

A loud, rumbling bark broke through the fog smothering Chet's brain, and he straightened. Otto, his best friend's retired police dog, bounded down the hill. His mouth open, tongue flopping in the breeze. Tucker strode down behind him, a grim set to his wide mouth and a hard glint in his blue eyes.

Otto skidded to a stop in front of Chet, kicking up fallen leaves and dirt. He pushed his nose into the palm of Chet's hand and sat.

Lincoln patted his back then took a step back. "Hey, Tucker."

Tucker dipped his chin in greeting. "Don't mean to be a bother. Just thought Otto could be of assistance."

Chet ran a hand over the dog's furry black head. Otto may be officially retired as a police dog, but he could still do the job. His nose worked just fine. Even if an injury to his right leg made his gait a little unsteady.

"I'll take all the help I can get," Lincoln said.

Appreciation chipped away at the hardened edges of panic still fisted around Chet's psyche. "Thanks, man. Cruz is on his way. The body's at the morgue. Some uniforms are scouring the area, looking for anything that can help."

"And Mia?" Tucker asked.

Beating back the guilt for not having an answer, Chet shrugged. "She gave a statement then hung around. Brooke came and got her."

Understanding lit Tucker's eyes. As Chet's best friend, he was privy to every detail of what had happened in Chet's past. He also understood how difficult it was for Chet to open up—to dive into the pain of what had happened to his wife and child. Tucker didn't ask any more questions. Instead, he whistled, drawing Otto back to him, then whispered something in the dog's ear.

Otto pressed his nose to the ground, sniffing every inch he covered with Tucker walking close behind.

Chet watched Otto head back up to the trail then disappear before facing Lincoln. "Now what?"

Lincoln sighed. "We have everyone on this that we can spare. Cruz talked to the medical examiner about rushing an autopsy. I've secured the scene and been over every square inch, which you can attest to since you've watched my every move. Go home. Check on Mia. She was pretty shaken and doesn't have the same support system in place you do."

Lifting his eyes to the cluster of green leaves overhead, Chet fisted his hands at his sides. Mia wasn't his problem. He had a shitload of emotions brewing inside him— emotions he kept a tight lid on day in and day out in order to survive—and he couldn't handle taking on someone else's trauma. Not when his own nearly swallowed him alive. "She's got Brooke."

Lincoln leveled a hard stare his way. "And when she goes home tonight, scared and alone, she'll have no one. You don't need to be her best friend. Just let her know you're around. Look out for her."

Chet scowled, not needing to be told what to do by some guy he barely knew. He didn't need to stop by Mia's apartment for a chat for her to know he was around. The walls were so damn thin she'd know the minute he was home. Not to mention she despised him as much as he was annoyed by her. She was better off having Brooke look after her.

A loud howl carried through the air, straightening Chet's spine. *Otto.* He took off at a sprint, his feet sticking to the hardening mud on the steep ravine. Weeds snaked up and grazed his jeans. Lincoln's heavy footsteps fell behind him, but he didn't spare him a glance as he traced the path Otto and Tucker had taken moments before.

"Over here," Tucker yelled, waving an arm in the air. The black ink circling his bicep peeked out from his gray t-shirt. "Tread lightly."

Chet changed directions, taking care to watch each step. Otto had led Tucker to a clearing in the woods, fifty yards or so from where the other officers fanned out. He kept his gaze latched on the giant black dog whose tail wagged and paws moved over unseen Earth. A cold sweat broke out on the back of his neck and the loud thud of his heart slamming against his breastbone blocked out the sound of the afternoon. "What is it?" He asked, halting a few yards away.

Tucker's deep frown set him on edge. "Otto found another body. This spot isn't just a random dumping ground. We're standing in the middle of a freaking cemetery."

3

The sun hung low in the sky, the full branches of the towering trees blocking out the retreating rays of warmth. A subtle breeze shifted the leaves and lifted the damp smell of unturned earth and fresh dirt to Chet's spot on the porch. Dried sweat ringed his short-sleeved T-shirt, his flannel draped over the porch railing.

A half-filled glass of whiskey nestled in his palm as he watched the parade of people and vehicles deserting the field of horrors they'd spent all day uncovering—leaving behind a lifetime of broken dreams and empty graves. Six women had been found. Six lives cut short and left to rot. Six arms burned with the same symbol he was forced to see every single day.

The screen door squeaked beside him and grated on his nerves. How hard was it for Mia to grab some oil to put on the hinges? He could offer to do it, but he didn't want her depending on him—asking him to help fix little problems in her apartment. He couldn't be responsible for someone else. Not again.

Hesitant footsteps skittered on the worn planks. Mia

stood in front of her door, huddled in an oversized hoodie to fight off the slight coolness. "What did they find?" She didn't turn toward him when she spoke, but kept her attention fixed on the retreating barrage of police vehicles and unmarked cars.

"Four more bodies." Fatigue and anger made his drawl more pronounced, his voice lower. "Six total."

Mia faced him, alarm widening her brown eyes. "This can't be happening."

Lifting his glass to his lips, he took a sip of the potent liquor. He savored the warmth that blazed down his esophagus. That same thought had consumed him years before, leaving him numb and unable to deal with the world. "Bad shit happens all the time."

Her jaw dropped for a beat before she snapped her mouth closed. "Not like this." She waved a hand toward the taillights blazing down the road. "Not bodies being uncovered so close to my home. And those poor women. Did the police say anything about how long they'd been there?"

He shrugged and swirled the ice in his glass. "Wouldn't say much." His previous experience on the force made him aware that Lincoln and Cruz wouldn't willingly tell him a lot about an ongoing investigation, but that didn't mean he hadn't hounded them until they'd finally forced him to leave. A bitter taste flooded his mouth, competing with the pungent aftertaste of the whiskey. Civilian or not, he needed to be a part of this case. He just had to figure out how.

Irritation twisted the delicate features of Mia's face. "That seems to be an ongoing problem around here."

He took another swig of whisky, weighing his words. But when none came, he simply shrugged and stared at the now quiet scene of the mountains.

"Am I that big of a pain in your ass that you can't shed

one ounce of compassion?" Her voice cracked and she raked a palm over her forehead. "I'm sorry if the world has hardened you so much that you can't offer a kind word or pass me a tiny bit of information. But damnit, I'm a wreck and just need something. Anything to help me sleep tonight. To comfort me as I lay in bed and try my hardest to unsee everything from today."

A humorless snort puffed from his nose. "I have no comfort to offer. No words to erase what happened today. If I had either, I'd give them." Putting one foot in front of the other was hard enough, he didn't have the energy to offer anything to anyone else.

"Do you hate me that much?" She asked, frowning.

The hurt in her tone was like a punch in the gut. He glanced up to meet her eyes, and the tears shimmering above her lashes fisted his throat. "I don't hate you."

Her dark brows dipped low, almost connecting at the narrow bridge of her nose. "Then tell me what I'm supposed to do. How I'm supposed to move on from this."

He worked his jaw back and forth as he stared at her. Had someone told her about his family? "Why would I know the answers to that? What have people told you?"

She hugged her middle, making the thick gray sweatshirt wrap tighter around her slim frame. "You were a police officer, right? I'm sure you've dealt with traumatizing situations."

He threw back the rest of his drink and stood. "You go to bed, wake up, and get on with your day. Then you do it all over again."

"And what about them?" She shivered and stared into the distance—stared into the far off place where bodies had been laid to rest.

A sharp jab of pain beat against his temples. This was a conversation he didn't want to be stuck in. "The police will try and identify the victims then notify their families."

She bobbed her head, as if in silent agreement with the process. "Hopefully knowing they've been found will help the families. Even if only a little."

He tightened his grip on the empty glass and fought the urge to throw it against the side of the cabin. He knew exactly what had happened to his wife and child and that knowledge didn't do a damn thing to help ease the pain. If nothing else, it made the agony burn so much brighter.

"I feel like I'm a part of this now," she said. "I want to help. Is that stupid?"

Sighing, he made his way to the door. Eager to end their little chat and down another glass—or two—of whiskey before falling into bed. "Not at all. It's normal."

"Is there anything I can do?"

"Not really. Cruz and Lincoln will tell you they've got it under control. That they can handle it."

She widened her eyes. "But they do, right? They'll find whoever did this?"

He wanted to laugh, to scream, to cry out that sometimes killers walked away. That sometimes it didn't matter how much people wanted to help, the bad guy slipped through the cracks and slinked into the shadows—waiting to strike again.

But the fear radiating from Mia made him bite his tongue. She'd seen an ugly part of reality that no one should ever see. He didn't have the heart to expose anymore unwanted truths. "I hope so." He reached for the door handle.

"What if they don't?"

The same question ate away at him. He turned toward her, hating the way the soft glow of dusk made her skin shimmer. "Then I will."

Mia sucked in a deep breath, filling her lungs with the sweetly scented air. Hints of vanilla and cinnamon mingled with her second cup of coffee—the first gulped down on her way into work this morning. Caffeine might zip through her veins, but it did nothing to keep her brain alert.

Something she needed when getting breakfast ready for a dozen guests at Crossroads Mountain Retreat.

The door from the dining room swung open and smashed against the wall. "Something's burning." Chet barked the statement and hurried to the stove, yanking open the oven door.

Frowning, she crossed over the black and white tiled floor and peered over his shoulder. The cinnamon buns rose perfectly, a golden-brown sheen showcasing their doneness. "Looks good to me."

Chet grabbed an oven mitt from the marble counter and pulled out the tray, tossing it on top of the stainless-steel oven. The tray teetered on the gray burners. "A minute more and they'd be ruined. You need to pay better attention."

The familiar bite of his criticism made her wince. Normally, she'd roll her eyes and move to her next task, but this morning her nerves were too tight—her emotions too raw. "I have enough on my mind this morning without you snapping at me." She shoved him out of the way and swiped a glazed-covered pastry brush over the buns.

He stayed close, her wimpy push barely moving him

from his place. Irritation rolled off him in waves, mixing with the heat from the oven. "I don't snap."

"Please," she said, taking care to apply an even coating of the sticky goodness. "That's all you ever do. It's like no one ever taught you how to speak to people." She shot him a glare over her shoulder before refocusing on her task. Watching the icing melt into the warm, sweet bread eased a bit of the tension pulling her muscles.

The kitchen door swung open, and Zoe Peyton waltzed in. The yoga instructor led daily classes at the retreat, as well as running her own studio in town, and had quickly become a friend to Mia. Her frequent pop-ins were a welcome distraction from Chet's sour disposition. A disposition that never seemed to rattle the tall, willowy woman, who just fixed a patient smile on her face and busied herself wherever needed.

"Morning," Zoe said, the usual chipperness gone from her voice.

Chet swiveled her way, eyes wide and expecting. "Cruz have any more information?"

Mia halted the motion of the pastry brush. Chances were low Zoe's boyfriend would give her information on an ongoing investigation, but she held her breath on the off chance she was wrong.

Frowning, Zoe made a beeline to the sink and washed her hands. "You know he doesn't talk to me about this stuff."

A low grumble vibrated from Chet's chest. "Come on, Zoe. Is there *anything* you can tell me? Something you over-heard or accidentally read in a file Cruz left on the table?"

"What kind of person do you think I am?" Zoe shot him a look then focused on Mia. "How are you?"

She shrugged. "As good as can be expected."

"If you need someone to talk to, I'm here. You could even come with me to the studio after breakfast if you don't want to be alone today. I won't even charge you for taking a class." Zoe winked and offered a small smile.

"Seriously?" Chet rubbed his fingers in circles over his temples. "You're joking right now? I need to know what's going on. I can't just stand here and pretend like nothing happened—that it's just another day."

Anger at his irritation with Zoe swirled in Mia's stomach. Before she could open her mouth, Zoe crossed the room and threw her arms around Chet's middle.

Chet stiffened, his hands balled into fists at his sides. "Zoe, don't—"

"Shut up and hug me, you big ass."

Chet's arms closed around Zoe, and his body relaxed.

An awkward silence lingered in the air, as if Mia was witnessing something she wasn't meant to see. She turned her back to Zoe and Chet but couldn't stop from hearing their murmured exchange.

"This sucks," Zoe said in a quiet, soothing voice. "You've been dealt a really shitty hand. We both know Cruz and Lincoln will do whatever they can to figure out who's responsible. You just need to let them do their job and not be a dick to everyone in the meantime."

Chet snorted.

"Things are mostly done here. Head on home, and Mia and I will finish up. Call Cruz. He'll tell you what he can."

Mia glanced behind her just as Chet dropped his arms from Zoe and swung her way. Their gazes locked, and for an instant, she saw a world of pain swimming in the depths of his eyes. Questions burned her tongue, but a scowl crumpled his mouth and he stormed away before she could voice a single one.

"Okay," Zoe said, swiping a platter of sliced fruit from the island. "I'll start taking everything out and setting up the buffet."

Mia blinked quickly. Confusion knitted her brow. Chet's behavior since yesterday was gruffer than usual, which she hadn't thought possible. She understood being upset, but the amount of pain and anger radiating from him made her reaction almost nonexistent in comparison.

Not wanting to dive into the complexity of Chet's brain, she busied herself with lining up the breakfast items as Zoe ferried them to the dining room. By the time breakfast was served and the mess cleaned, Mia's curiosity had fanned the flames of her imagination. She dried the last dish, putting it in its place, and casually asked, "So what's going on with Chet? I'm surprised to see him so upset."

Zoe wiped off the counter then tossed the dirty towel in a bin stored under the sink. "Chet's story isn't for the faint of heart, and it's not mine to tell."

Mia swished her mouth to the side, hesitation slowing her words. She didn't want to snoop but her mind spun with reasons for Chet's odd behavior. "I promise I'm not a gossip. It's just that I've worked here for months now and can't put my finger on that guy. He can be such an ass and has never given me a fair chance. Never been happy to have me here. Now, on top of that, he's so shaken. I guess his reaction is just surprising, and I'm trying to understand."

"I get it," Zoe said. "I really do. Being around Chet can be difficult, but he's been through a lot. Maybe you should ask him about it. Having an honest conversation might clear the air. Now come on. I have a class in twenty minutes." She wiggled her fingers in a come-here motion until Mia met her by the door. Zoe circled an arm around Mia's shoulders and gave a little squeeze.

Brooke's statement from the morning before echoed in Mia's head. She'd mentioned Chet's demons, and now this morning's interaction between Chet and Zoe made her wonder if there was more to the giant pain in her backside. Maybe there was a reason Chet was so difficult, but even if there was, it didn't matter. She still didn't deserve to be treated like dirt and didn't have the desire to peel back the layers of any man. Not after what she'd been through.

As she walked down the hall and into the lobby with its warm wood beams running along the high-pitched ceiling and three-story stone hearth that anchored the room, she vowed to stick to her plan. It didn't matter that things took a horrible turn and she'd uncovered a plethora of graves near her home, or that she realized there was more to Chet than met the eye. She'd keep showing up to a job she loved and keeping her eye on the future—putting away money and saving for the restaurant she'd always wanted.

A restaurant that had been within her grasp until her good-for-nothing ex took everything and ran.

"Do you want to drive into town with me?" Zoe asked as she pushed out the door and stepped onto the wide porch.

A warm breeze brushed against Mia's cheek and cooled her heated skin. She hadn't told Zoe she'd even go with her, but yoga sounded better than sitting home alone. "I'll drive and meet you."

"See you there." Zoe waved then hurried to her car.

Mia lifted a palm and watched Zoe drive out of the small parking lot at the front of the lodge. She took a second to appreciate the explosion of trees and wildflowers crowding the perimeter of the stone lot before heading toward her car. Gravel crunched under her feet. She fished her hand into the purse dangling from her shoulder in search of her keys then stopped short. Her heartbeat doubled its rhythm, the rush of blood making her head spin. Shock rooted her feet to the spot.

Deep slits ripped through her tires, a knife left in the rubber of the front wheel.

4

Swelling clouds rolled through the bruised sky as Chet jumped from his truck and hurried into the police station before the rain started. Screw calling Cruz. It'd be a lot harder for Cruz or Lincoln or any other officer working the case to brush him aside if he was in their faces. The brick building stood at the edge of the town square. He swung open the door, and the deep frown on his face must have convinced the young officer to buzz him through without asking questions.

Not like the guy didn't know who Chet was. Hell, he probably understood exactly why he was here. The young officer had been a fresh-faced police academy graduate when Chet was on the force, and he appreciated still being treated like one of the team.

Dipping his head in a silent greeting, he stepped into the gentle hum of the main section of the station. Where desks scattered along the tanned, carpeted floor. He scanned the open space, spotting Cruz in one of only two offices squeezed inside the station, a phone pressed against his ear and fatigue written on every line of his face.

Chet halted outside the open door, not wanting to interrupt Cruz's conversation.

Cruz waved him inside and pointed a finger at one of two chairs on the opposite side of the desk then mouthed, 'Close the door'.

Chet complied then plopped into the empty chair. He rested his elbow on the arm then let his head fall into his hand. He closed his eyes, needing a second to pull himself together while also listening in to Cruz's call, hoping to hear something of interest.

"How ya holding up, man?"

Chet opened his eyes to find Cruz staring at him, the receiver nestled into the old-fashioned phone at the corner of his desk. He scrubbed his palms over his cheeks. "Shit. I think I just fell asleep."

"Feel free to take a nap." Cruz grabbed a manilla file from the top of his closed laptop and flipped it open. "But I have a feeling you'll want to see this." Slipping a paper from the file, he passed it over the oak desk.

Leaning forward, Chet snatched the paper and studied an image of a young woman with long blond hair and a warm smile. "This is the girl from the grave." The skin tone was lighter and the blue of her wide-set eyes more vivid, but there was no mistaking who he was looking at.

"Janie Simpson. Reported missing two days ago. From Knoxville. Does she look familiar to you at all?"

The unexpected question knocked him off balance and took him right back to three years before when police threw more than one curveball his way as they searched for Laurie and Riley's killer. At the time of their deaths, only one other branded victim had been found. Shelly Preston. Investigators had searched for any possible connections between his family and the unlucky woman who'd been murdered two weeks before his living night-mare began.

"No." He laid the photo back on the desk. "Have you learned much about her?"

Cruz shook his head. "Just ID'd her this morning. I talked to her family earlier. Damn, that was brutal."

Unwanted memories assaulted Chet. He couldn't go back to that place—to that time. Back to notifications and autopsy reports. Only to remember every excruciating detail after he'd been released from the hospital, forced to replay every second in his mind. Forced to wonder if he'd done something different, made a different choice or fought harder, if he could have saved his family.

But he had to go back to it. Had to remember it all and replay it over and over if he was going to help find the bastard responsible for taking so many lives, leaving count-less others beyond repair.

"How long was she in the grave?"

"Not long," Cruz said. "The crime scene unit is guessing an hour tops, possibly less. She hadn't been dead long."

A flash of alarm straightened his spine. "Could he have seen Mia?"

"It's possible. We searched every inch of terrain we could yesterday, and another team is out there right now before the rain hits. No trace of whoever dug that grave. The only thing we know is it was fresh. If Mia had started her hike earlier, she may have stumbled upon something much scarier than a hand."

"He might have heard her coming. Spooked him into running and leaving a half-ass job. There's a reason those other graves hadn't been found until now. Without Mia interrupting something, this grave could have faded into the unknown like the others."

Cruz shrugged. "It's possible, but no proof as of now to confirm anything."

Chet threaded his fingers through his beard, running scenarios through is head. "How did he get the body up there? I was sitting on the porch and would have seen if anyone had driven up the lane. It's private property. No parking lots or side streets to park on. And why would the killer bury the body first thing in the morning and not at night? He'd obviously been in the area before, doing the same despicable thing. He could have navigated the area at night."

"He might have panicked," Cruz said, tapping his finger on the edge of the desk. "Plans might have been screwed up. This is the first time we've got a whiff of this asshole since he vanished three years ago. He made a mistake when he left you alive in that house, and now he's made another one. This time, we will find him."

"Any idea how he found his victim?" Chet asked.

"Looks like he snatched her after one of her night classes. She was a student at Highpoint Community College."

A wave of dizziness sent his senses spinning, and he gripped the arms of the chair to center himself. "Professor Lipton."

"Doesn't mean anything." Cruz held up a hand, a deep frown squaring off his jaw. "Just because it's the same college."

Anger and frustration shot Chet to his feet. "Are you kidding me? He was the last person to see my wife before she went missing. The last person she talked to. He was always inappropriate, never hid his interest in her. He told her to drop that stupid paper off in his office, after hours, and she took Riley with her. Then poof." He flicked his fingers in the air, mimicking an exploding bomb. "Gone until he brought them back to that damn house."

He'd been nothing but supportive and proud as hell when Laurie decided to go back to school for her masters. Teaching was her passion, and if furthering her education would set her career up for a better future, he was more than happy to help in any way he could. Never would he have imagined her fateful encounter with one of her professors would rip his family apart.

The police might not have proven Professor Lipton was the killer, but no other suspect came close to drawing the same suspicion. Having the same red flags.

"Did Janie Simpson have a class with the good professor?" The last words were spat out on a wave of venom and sarcasm.

"I'm digging into that now. I was on the phone with the college. The woman I spoke with agreed to send me all the information she has on Janie, including her class schedule."

"Can't wait to see what it says." He settled back into the seat and crossed his arms over his chest. He didn't care if Cruz wanted him here or not. His friend would have to physically remove him.

A sharp rap on the door sounded, and the young officer from the front desk stepped inside. "A call just went through to dispatch. They sent Lincoln up to Crossroads Mountain Retreat, but I thought you'd want to know what happened."

"What's going on? I was just there," Chet said, scooting to the edge of the seat.

"Mia Tulley called. Someone slit her tires. All four of them."

Chet rose as Cruz swore under his breath. The email would have to wait. Even though he hated the nagging urge to check on Mia, he had to follow it. She'd been dealt a tough blow the day before, and now someone had vandalized her car. No way in hell the two weren't connected. He might not want Mia to depend on him for a damn thing, but he couldn't leave her stranded. He'd check in on her, see what Lincoln thought of the situation, then find out what Cruz learned about Janie Simpson—forcing Mia back to the corner of his mind.

A place he vowed he'd always keep her.

MIA WATCHED as Officer Sawyer turned her old sedan into a crime scene. He'd placed the knife from her front passenger side tire in an evidence bag, dusted for prints, and was now assisting in loading the car onto the back of a tow truck.

Desperation made her stomach ache. She didn't have money to pay for four new tires, and she had no idea what her insurance would cover. Since she only carried minimum coverage, she assumed they wouldn't give her enough money to cover the cost of the wheels.

Brooke jogged down the porch steps and stopped at her side. Her pinched expression didn't bode well for what she'd found. "The camera doesn't catch anything this far out in the lot. I'm sorry."

"I guess it would have been too easy if the person responsible was caught on video." Mia wrapped her arms around her middle in a pathetic attempt to shield herself from some unseen threat. She searched the explosion of colors surrounding her that she'd admired not long ago. Dark shadows wove between thick tree trunks, providing the perfect cover for anyone lingering nearby.

But who? Who would want to slash her tires? And why?

The tow truck pulled out of the lot, and Officer Sawyer

offered Brooke a gentle smile before setting his mouth in a grim line. "I'm sorry about this, Mia."

"Where is he taking my car?" She asked, dipping her head toward the retreating truck as it turned out of sight.

"Down to the station. I did everything I can out here but want the crime scene unit to have a look. With what happened yesterday, I want to make sure to be as thorough as possible with your car. Bringing the vehicle to the station will keep anything—or anyone—else from messing with it until they have a chance to get to it. And with everything they're trying to get done at the grave sites, it might be a while before they get to the car." Officer Sawyer stared up at the rumbling sky. "Though with the rain coming, everyone will leave the woods. The water will wash away anything of use."

"You can use one of the golf carts to get around," Brooke said.

The retreat kept a fleet of golf carts on hand for the guests to drive to their cabins. The cabins were all nestled along the large, picturesque lake behind the lodge. Gravel trails traveled from different locations around the retreat. None of the trails or pathways were large enough for vehicles to navigate, so the carts were available for guests and staff to use.

Mia envisioned sliding down the rain-soaked, mountain road in a tiny death trap. "Not sure how safe I'd feel driving one of the golf carts home, but thanks for the offer."

"Then I'll take you anywhere you need to go until you get your car back." Brooke flashed a wide smile that didn't vanquish the worry in her eyes. "We'll make sure you have a way to get around."

A big, red truck turned into the parking lot, and Mia cringed. The last thing she wanted was another confrontation with Chet. He'd been crankier than usual while working this morning, the tension between them thicker than the growing clouds overhead.

Chet parked his car beside the cruiser and hopped down, his constant frown firmly in place on his handsome face. He held her gaze at he stormed forward, and it took all her strength not to break eye contact. "You okay?"

The tenderness of his usually gruff voice threw her off, and she nodded.

He dipped his chin then faced his friend. "What the hell happened? When I left earlier her car was fine."

Officer Sawyer rubbed the back of his neck. "Not sure. Obviously, someone wanted to mess with Mia. I need to figure out who and why."

"Do you think it's related to what happened yesterday?" Chet asked.

The question sent a shudder down Mia's spine. The eerie sensation of being watched had followed her home from the woods yesterday, but she'd assumed she was being paranoid. Could someone really have seen her? Followed her to work then slashed her tires to send some kind of sick message? The thought of it made her stomach churn.

"I don't know, but I'll damn sure find out," Officer Sawyer said.

"Do you want me to drive you home?" Brooke asked.

Mia's mind spun. Her life hadn't exactly been rainbows and sunshine the last few months, but how had it spiraled into worst case scenario so fast? Needing a second to think things through, she pinched the bridge of her nose. "I can just hang here. I need to come back to serve lunch anyway, and if I go home I won't have a way back."

Brooke cupped her palm on Mia's bicep, her brows

dipped in concern. "Don't worry about lunch, or dinner for that matter. Let me take you home, and you can relax."

Laughter bubbled in her throat. Brooke meant well, but how was she supposed to relax? A plop of rain landed on her forehead, and she wiped it away. She struggled for a response, a thought, a damn sentence to explain what she wanted right now, but no words came. Her nerve endings danced a tango and the idea of being alone scared her more than she wanted to admit. But she didn't want to burden her employer and reject her generosity.

"I'll take her," Chet said, fisting his keys. "I'm heading there anyway. No need to waste anyone else's time."

The punch of gratitude for his offer warred with her desperate desire not to spend time trapped in a truck alone with Chet. The drops of rain grew larger, and she let them slide down her face. "Are you sure?"

"Yep." Without waiting for her answer, he marched back to his truck and started the engine.

"Guess I'm going with Chet. Thanks for everything, Officer."

"I think it's time you call me Lincoln," he said with a snort. "I'll be in touch soon about your vehicle."

She nodded her thanks, waved goodbye, then headed for the truck—her steps heavy with dread. The drive home was no more than ten minutes, but she had a feeling it would be the longest drive of her life.

5

By the time Mia sprinted the short distance to Chet's idling truck, the sky had opened and rain pelted down. Water dripped from the ends of her dark hair and her blue t-shirt clung to her body—the stiff, wet denim of her jeans heavy and uncomfortable.

Chet might have missed the downpour, but moisture from the earlier sputter of rain mussed his brown hair, spiking it in wayward peaks. He peeled off his ever-present flannel, exposing bulging muscles under his gray shirt, then tossed the discarded clothing between them on the bench seat.

Mia kept her focus out the windshield as Chet swung onto the narrow mountain road, the wipers swinging back and forth in a flurry of motion. Temptation to ogle the chiseled body he always kept hidden under his stupid flannel had her tightening her jaw. The last thing she needed was to be impressed by any part of her neighbor. His handsome face was already annoying enough. "Thanks for the ride," she said, needing to fill the quiet space with more than tension and the sound of swooshing wipers.

"No problem."

More awkward silence pulsed between them. Mia clenched her hands together in her lap. Needing to expel the nervous energy zipping through her body, she crossed her legs then wiggled her dangling foot. "I don't know what I'm going to do without my car."

"Lincoln shouldn't have it long."

She waited for him to say more, unsurprised when he didn't. Conversation wasn't his strong suit on a good day. "Even when I get it back, I can't buy new tires." She blurted out the words, rambling as the car slowed to round a sharp curve in the road. She wanted to ask who he thought could have done something like this but was afraid of the answer. "I'll call my insurance company, but I'm not expecting much. Is there a cheap place around here I can get some wheels?"

"Going cheap on tires isn't a good idea. Especially around here." He flicked his gaze in the rearview mirror then refocused ahead of him.

She rolled her eyes. "As if I have a choice."

He cast her a quick glance, his curiosity plain in his furrowed brow.

She shifted, his attention making her uncomfortable. She'd kept her reasons for moving to Pine Valley to herself, not even confiding in Brooke or Zoe. The last thing she wanted was to spill her most embarrassing mistake to Chet —expose how loving the wrong man left her without a penny to her name and a shattered heart.

Thick lines circling Chet's wrists caught her attention, and Zoe's earlier words came back to her. Maybe if she wanted Chet to tell her his story, she should be more open about hers. She weighed her options before deciding to open up a little. What could the truth of her situation do? Make their relationship worse?

Slumping her head against the back of her seat, she sighed. "My ex-boyfriend emptied out my savings. He took everything from me. That's why I moved here. To start over and build back the life he stole. If I want to make rent next month, I'll have to go bare bones on the tires."

"I'm sorry." The grunted words grumbled from deep in his throat and practically made the air vibrate. "Guy sounds like an ass."

She snorted out a laugh and turned her head to face him. As much as she hated talking about Aaron, it was nice to focus on more normal aspects of her life. No matter how depressing they were. "Ass might be an understatement."

"Why Pine Valley?" he asked.

His interest caught her off guard. "I don't really know. I like the small town. And Brooke needed a kitchen assistant. I've always wanted to own a restaurant, so it seemed like a good place to gain experience."

"I didn't need any help."

She shook her head in irritation. He made it so difficult to have a conversation. "Well, Brooke didn't agree. So here I am."

"Hmm," he said as his phone rang from his pocket. He yanked it out, flipping open the phone then pressing it to his ear.

She suppressed a giggle. Who still used a flip phone? As he listened to whoever was on the other line, she let her gaze travel from the large hand pressing the phone to his ear down to the scars on his wrist and up the corded muscles of his forearm.

Her blood turned cold.

A circular scar with intricate loops marred the inside of his arm inches below his elbow. The skin was raised, the symbol an eerie white. The same scar she'd seen on the woman in the grave yesterday. Hard knots looped together in her chest, pushing against her organs and making it hard to breathe. Chet's voice droned on, sounding far away in her ringing ears.

Why did he have a matching mark carved on his arm? What could it mean? Who put it there? Could Chet be the one who branded himself, then used the same disgusting symbol on the women he killed then buried not far from his own home?

Fear strangled her, and she grabbed hold of the door handle. Preparing to launch herself from the moving car if necessary.

"Mia?"

She forced down the saliva pooling in her throat. Her heart pumped wildly, making her head spin.

"Mia! What's wrong?"

Licking her lips, she tore her gaze from his arm and met his confused stare.

Red slashed across his face, and he tightened his jaw. "Just ask the damn question."

The gentleness from before was gone from his gruff tone, and she flinched. "Wh—what do you mean?"

"Don't act like you don't know what I'm talking about." He dipped his chin toward his arm. "You saw it. Now spill whatever questions are churning in that brain of yours."

She kept her hand curved around the handle. "Where did you get that mark?"

"My guess is the same man who put it on my arm is the one who killed the girl you found. The same man who killed my family."

Her mouth went dry, and shame heated her ears. Her

mind had pinned him as a killer, a monster, someone to be afraid of. She'd never imagined he was a victim, or that something so horrible could have happened to him. She waited for him to say more, to explain, but the suffocating silence came back.

Chet pulled into the driveway that led to the duplex.

She bit her lip, determined not to ask more questions. If he wanted to tell her more, he would. And something so traumatic wouldn't be easy for anyone to talk about. Especially Chet.

As Chet parked the truck, a man stood from a wooden rocking chair on the porch. Her insides twisted as he waited and watched. His stare latched onto the truck, his hands shoved into the pockets of his trousers.

Mia steeled her resolve. Chet might not be the monster she'd imaged a few moments before, but she had no clue who this man was. She'd run like hell if she had to, do whatever it took to survive.

CHET BIT back a groan at the unexpected visitor. Eddy Truly was a nice enough guy, but Chet's patience was running pretty damn low. But he'd grab hold of any excuse to get some distance from Mia. The mix of shock and panic on her face when she'd spotted his scar had set him on edge. Discussing his past was low on his list of fun tasks, but he'd assumed it'd come up with Mia after what happened yesterday.

Now that he'd blurted out a part of his pain, he wanted to get as far away from the pity that swam in her dark eyes as possible.

Without sparing Mia another glance, he dashed out of

the truck. The rain pelted him, but the coolness of the water centered him—brought him back to reality. Back to the present moment. Pounding up the steps, he ran a hand through his strands to shake out the moisture. "Hey, Eddy. What's up?"

Eddy extended a hand, waiting for Chet to place his palm in his before giving it a shake. "Just checking in."

The sound of a car door slamming echoed through the air. Mia ran through the sheet of rain, landing on the wooden planks of the porch with soaked hair and wide eyes.

"You must be Mia," Eddy said, aiming a small smile her way. He dipped his chin but kept his hands to his side.

She pinched her smooth brow together and nodded. "I am. And you are?"

The end of her sentence shook with what sounded like fear, and Chet mentally slapped himself for not telling Mia who Eddy was as soon as he spotted him on the porch. After everything she'd been through, a stranger waiting for her to get home must have been alarming.

"This is Bobby's nephew, Eddy," Chet said. "He's run Truly's Trading Post since Bobby retired." Truly's Trading Post was the local general store. Bobby's grandfather had started the trading post when the town was first settled, providing the citizens with odds and ends they needed on their homesteads. Through the years, the store had turned into more of a modern hardware store, adding a few novelties to compete with the online competitors and big box stores in the larger, surrounding towns.

"Retired's a bit of a loose term with Uncle Bobby, but at least Aunt Missy got him to take her on that cruise." Eddy went back to his place against the porch railing. His ginger hair curled just over his ears, falling to the nape of his neck. Black-framed glasses hid prominent eyebrows.

"It's nice to meet you," Mia said. "I adore your uncle."

"Most people do," Eddy said. "He's a bit of a staple in Pine Valley."

"What brings you here?" Chet asked, cutting to the chase. He'd rather put a fork in his eye than make small talk, and Eddy had a habit of sticking around where he wasn't wanted. Like a stray cat who never leaves after a do-gooder left out a bowl of tuna.

Not to mention the conversation from his earlier phone call with Cruz still spun in his head. Janie Simpson had taken a class with Professor Lipton. Now Chet had to prove the man was the one they were after. To do that, he needed to get rid of Eddy so he could pour through all the notes he still had from his wife and daughter's case.

Eddy's goofy grin fell. "Cruz called Uncle Bobby and filled him in on what happened yesterday. He's so upset. He wants to come home early, but Aunt Missy will throw a fit. It's taken her years to get him to leave town. You know how he is. Always toting around that toolbox, helping folks around town. Doesn't think anyone can make it without him."

Chet's patience thinned, and he rolled his finger in a circle to indicate Eddy needed to wrap it up.

A light red tinted Eddy's pale face. "Sorry. I told Uncle Bobby I'd stop by. See how you two are doing." He dipped his chin toward Mia then him. "Told him I'd talk to the police and help out with anything I can. You know, gotta do what I can do save a fifty-plus year marriage."

"That's very thoughtful of you," Mia said, offering a warm smile.

"We're fine," Chet growled, not liking the way Eddy straightened when Mia looked at him. Not liking the jealousy blooming in his chest because Mia never smiled at him like that. "I'm sure Cruz will appreciate any assistance. He's down at the station."

Eddy nodded, the hint that it was time to leave going over his head.

A silver truck turned down the driveway and swayed as it bounced on the deep ruts in the gravel.

Mia lifted on her toes. "Who's that?"

Chet blew out a frustrated breath. It was like Grand Central Station here today. "Tucker." He tapped the tip of his booted foot on the floor, dragging his fingertips over the raised edges of the scars circling his wrist.

Tucker parked the truck then hopped out, waiting to close the door until Otto jumped down.

Otto barked then ran to the porch, a slight limp in his gait. With his tail wagging, he pressed his nose to the ground and headed straight for Eddy. He sniffed Eddy's shoes then pressed his head against the hardware store owner's hand.

Eddy tensed and lifted his palms, as if afraid Otto would bite.

Tucker lumbered up the steps and grinned. "You know he wouldn't hurt a fly, Eddy."

Eddy cringed. "And you know I'll never like dogs. Not after what happened when we were kids."

Mia dropped to a crouch and clapped her hands. "Come here, boy. I'll give you some love."

Otto charged Mia with his tongue hanging from his mouth and what Chet swore was a damn smile on his dopey face.

"I'm going to head out," Eddy said, backing up. "Glad you're okay. Call me if you need anything. I'll go to the station to see Cruz. Tucker, good to see you, man."

"You, too, buddy."

Chet waited until Eddy was out of earshot. "Got rid of one of you, now what do *you* want?" He didn't have to look at Tucker for his friend to understand who he was talking to.

Tucker ran a palm over Otto's head then opened the door to Chet's side of the duplex. "I just talked to Cruz. Let's head in. The rain's getting heavier. Won't be long before the wind shifts and blows the water right at us."

Chet groaned, knowing he wouldn't get rid of his friend as easily as he had Eddy. "Fine."

Mia stood. "Thanks again for the ride." She bit into her bottom lip, hesitation clear in her slow movement toward her own door.

"Otto insists you come in here with us," Tucker said, taking a step inside.

Mia connected her gaze with Chet, brows hooked high as if asking his permission.

He swept a hand through the air, gesturing her to proceed him into the apartment. "Might as well join us." He waited for her to enter his home, the dog at her heels, then rubbed the back of his neck. So much for his solitude.

6

Warm earth tones and an almost OCD type of cleanliness rooted Mia to her spot right inside Chet's doorway. She might have lived directly next door for the last few months, but she'd never stepped foot in his home. She'd imagined messy clutter and a giant stuffed Grizzly bear in the corner. Not cozy furniture nestled around a stone fireplace with an underlying scent of lemon disinfectant in the air.

A light touch between her shoulder blades made her jump. "You gonna go in?"

Chet's husky voice skimmed the back of her neck, making the hairs stand on end. The feel of his hand against her thin shirt heated her skin and stole her composure. "Oh, I'm sorry." She stepped to the side and let him slide past her.

"Come on, Tuck. Take your damn shoes off," Chet said, sliding his boots off and setting them on a black mat by the door. "Did you even wipe Otto's paws?"

The muddy prints marring the oak floors were answer enough. She braced herself for Chet's roar of reprimand she often received at work, but instead, he chuckled then grabbed a rag from the kitchen and mopped up the mess.

Mia stepped out of her sneakers and stood in her socked-feet, feeling awkward. She should have just gone back to her place, but the idea of sitting alone in her empty house made unease settle in her gut. She couldn't avoid being by herself forever, but she'd put it off as long as possible. Even if it meant being uncomfortable in Chet's home.

After getting his paws wiped by Chet, Otto trotted to her side. Thank God for the dog. If nothing else, she could dote on him. She surveyed the space as she pet his soft fur. The room was open, just like on her side of the wall. A small living area connected to the kitchen with a hallway leading to the back of the apartment. Warm, wooden beams criss-crossed the high ceiling, contrasted by the cool slab of granite on the counter taking over the far wall in the kitchen. An olive-green rug anchored the living room with inviting furniture facing the fireplace.

But no knick-knacks sat on the counters or photos lined the walls. Her own space didn't boast much beyond a two-person table, worn sofa and coffee table, but she'd surrounded herself with pictures of her family and fond memories of her childhood. Things that made her smile. Made her feel like she was home.

Tucker kicked his shoes into a corner and plopped on a kitchen chair. "Take a seat, Mia."

"I'm fine over here with Otto." She kneeled on the ground to get closer to the dog. "You know how much I love this guy."

Tucker worked at the retreat and handled the therapy dogs. He managed an entire kennel filled with retired canines from K-9 units around the area who didn't have handlers to take care of them after they couldn't work. All the dogs were given proper training and now worked to help soothe some of the residents at the retreat. Most days she had more time on her hands than she knew what to do with, so she wandered down to the kennel to spend time with the dogs.

"The feeling's mutual," Tucker said. "Most of the dogs probably prefer you. Always giving them walks and filling their dishes. I'm the one left to do the training."

As if to prove his owner right, Otto flipped onto his back and exposed his stomach.

Mia chuckled and scrubbed the soft skin of his tummy.

Chet grunted and filled the coffee pot. "Dog likes anyone who gives him attention. Why are you here Tucker?"

"Cruz told me about Mia's tires."

"What else did he tell you?" Keeping his back to them, Chet grabbed three mugs from the cabinet and set them on the counter.

"He told me about Professor Lipton."

Mia's ears perked up at the familiar name. "The guy who teaches at High Point Community College?"

Chet spun around. "Excuse me?"

Mia stood, unsure of what she'd said to cause such heat in Chet's brown eyes. She bounced her gaze between him and Tucker then back to Chet. "What?"

"You know Professor Lipton?"

She shrugged. "I took a couple of classes last year. Business classes." At the time, she'd finally scrimped and saved enough money that she could actually envision her dream becoming a reality. She had the skills in the kitchen, but she'd wanted to have more confidence in the business side of things. Taking a few classes at the college helped with that.

Tucker stood and swiped a mug then filled it from the

now-full pot. "Let's all head to the living room. Mia, want a cup?"

Unexpected tension sizzled in the air. "Umm, sure. Just black is fine." She waited for Tucker to bring her an oversized sky-blue mug then followed him to the couch, Otto padding along behind her.

Chet paced in the kitchen, muttering to himself. His empty mug forgotten on the counter.

She cupped her hands around the warm mug, afraid to spill a drop in the spotless home. "What's going on?"

Tucker took a sip of coffee, brows raised as he watched Chet. "You gonna tell her? Or do you want me to?"

She tried to keep up with the unspoken conversation between them, but her mind trudged along, falling further behind with every second.

Chet stopped pacing and planted his feet hip-width apart, his broad chest heaving in and out as if he struggled to catch his breath. "The woman who you found yesterday took classes at the college, and Cruz just found out she took one of Professor Lipton's classes."

Unable to stomach the acidic brew, Mia set her untouched drink on a narrow table beside the brown, suede couch. "Okay. I'm sure a lot of young women have taken his class. If I remember correctly, he'd taught there for quite a while."

"My wife also took one of his classes." Chet clenched his teeth, the intense squared off jaw sharp even under his full beard. "He was the last person to see her alive." His voice cracked, and he hung his head.

Her heart splintered in two. He hadn't confided much beyond the fact his family had been killed. Now he was telling her that a man she knew, that she actually liked and respected, was the last person to see his wife. She weighed her words carefully, wanting answers but not wanting to offend. "If he was the last person to see her, I'd assume the police questioned him."

"They did," Tucker said, slowly. Carefully. As if he too was afraid to say anything that would trigger Chet's temper. "Even though some things didn't add up, they didn't have enough to charge him."

"And now another woman who is dead is connected to him, and so is a woman whose tires were just slashed. If he saw you in the woods yesterday, would he have recognized you?" Chet asked, tilting his head as he studied her.

A lump lodged in her throat, the answer stuck in a wave of terror. She nodded. "What does that mean?"

Chet stomped over to a small desk wedged beside the door and pulled a thick file from a drawer. "Three strikes against Professor Lipton means he still looks guilty as hell. Now all I have to do is prove it."

HANDWRITTEN NOTES and glossy photos stared up at Chet from the file he'd shoved in a drawer years before and refused to take out. Reminders of the past he'd never forget but didn't need to face. Just like now, he'd never officially been part of the investigation that failed to find the man who murdered his family.

And just like before, nothing would stop him from diving in head first. But this time, he'd finally see justice served. Life would never be the same, he'd never get back what he'd lost, but making sure the madman who'd taken so much from so many was punished had to give him at least a shred of peace.

Flipping open the file on the kitchen table, he ignored

the two people staring at him from his living room. He spread out papers, each one like a punch in the gut. Each piece of evidence or theory he'd concocted twisted his insides a little bit more.

The sound of a chair scraping against the floor drew his attention to Tucker. He sat, placing his mug of steaming coffee on an empty space on the table. "You sure you want to do this? Cruz and Lincoln are more than capable. You don't need to be sucked back in." He flicked a wrist over the mess of contents.

"I'm sure."

"They're not going to like it. Cruz might be willing to throw you bits of information when he can, even asking your opinion based on what happened to Laurie and Riley. But he's not going to want you working beside them, especially Lincoln. He's new around here. He won't understand like Cruz does."

Chet lifted his gaze and met Tucker's stare head on. "Like that's going to stop me."

"All right then." Tucker rubbed his palms together. "Let's dive in. I'm by your side, buddy. Whatever you need. Whenever you need it."

Mia cleared her throat.

With his fists planted on the table, he swiveled his face toward her. She stood closer than he expected, her arms crossed loosely around her middle and one ankle hooked over the other. A small pout of her lips showcased her self-consciousness. Otto stayed glued to her side. "Do you want me to leave?"

A part of him wanted her to go home because he couldn't think as clear when she was so near. In his apartment. Looking as though she belonged there. But he couldn't say that, at least not when she might have some information that could be helpful. "How well do you know Professor Lipton?"

She ran her fingers through her still-damp hair, scrunching the wavy strands at the crown of her head and puffing them up. "Not well. I mean, it's not like you spend a whole lot of time with your professors outside of class. And in class, we stuck to discussing spreadsheets and how to write a business plan."

"Did he ever ask you personal questions?" Chet asked. "Ever make you feel uncomfortable?"

She shook her head. "Not that I recall."

Tucker pulled out the chair beside him. "Why don't you sit?"

She took the offered chair, leaning forward to look at all the papers Chet had dumped on the table. Her gaze landed on a photo of Laurie and Riley, and the muscles in Chet's neck tightened. He traced a finger along the glossy picture, over Laurie's long, blonde hair then over to the teddy bear Riley used to drag everywhere. His heart seized and unshed tears burned his eyes.

Damnit. This is why he didn't take pictures out—didn't look back on happier times. All it ever did was cause him pain.

"They were both so beautiful." Mia's whispers were barely audible over the ringing in his ears. "So young."

When Chet didn't say anything, Tucker offered her a small smile. "You're right on both accounts. Best damn girls I've ever met."

Needing to force all his suffering aside, he picked up the photo and shoved it back in the file. That was the picture the police had used when looking for his family. It was almost impossible to remember the day he'd captured that moment between his girls. A fun day on the lake. Sun streaking through their hair, laughter on their faces and in their matching green eyes. Now, that photo conjured up memories of flashing blue and red lights and a frantic need to find them.

"I'm sorry," Mia said, leaning back in her seat. "I didn't mean to upset you."

Chet squeezed his eyes closed for a second and shook his head. "Not your fault. But let's get back to Lipton. Is there anything at all you can tell me about the guy?"

She lifted one shoulder. "Not really."

Chet fell into the empty chair across from Tucker and pinched the thick skin of his forehead. "There's got to be something we missed before."

Mia tucked in her bottom lip as if unsure if she should voice any more of her opinions. "I don't have any experience with this stuff, but shouldn't you be looking at Janie? At her life and her family. Not just at the one aspect of her life that happened to intersect with your wife's." Otto plopped his head in her lap, and she scratched behind his ear.

"Why waste time?" Frustration pounded in his veins. He'd already been through one drawn out investigation that resulted in jack shit. He couldn't go through that again. This time, he'd do things his way. No matter who liked it or not.

"She's right, man." Tucker sifted through a handful of notes. "We keep our eyes on Lipton, ask what questions need to be asked, but don't box ourselves in. We need to find out more about Janie. And when the other victims are identified, we learn everything we can about them, too."

Chet threw his hands in the air, not wanting to listen to anyone else's logic. Even if it did make sense. "What if they can't identify anyone else? What if it takes days, months, freaking years to figure out who all was left out there to rot?"

Mia winced.

Tucker sighed and tossed the papers he was studying back on the table. "We still take a closer look at Janie. We pour over these notes, talk to Cruz and anyone else who worked that case, and we see if there are any other similarities. Two victims are enough to create a profile on the killer. To maybe get a better understanding of who he is, and why he picked these two victims."

"Three," Chet said, grinding together his teeth. "Three victims. Riley might not have been this guy's initial target, but she got caught up in it and ripped away just like Laurie."

An unreadable expression skittered across Mia's face, and she dropped down to hug Otto. "I think I should head home."

Her swift change of subject caught him off guard, but the idea of putting a wall between them loosened a few of the knots in his stomach. "You sure?"

"I need to get out of these wet clothes, and you guys have enough on your plate without babysitting me." She stood. "Thanks for letting me hang for a little bit."

Otto whined.

"We always like having you around," Tucker said. "But dry clothes will make you feel better. Why don't you take Otto for the night to keep you company?"

A flash of relief shone in her eyes. "Really?"

"Sure thing. I have some extra supplies in the truck for him. I'll drop them off when I'm done here."

"Thanks. For everything. I'll see you both later." Mia snapped her fingers, calling Otto to her, while she slipped on her shoes then hurried out the door.

A beat of regret rang through Chet as he watched her leave, knowing she'd be uneasy until this was all behind them. But he couldn't worry about her state of mind. She wasn't his responsibility, and he had bigger problems to focus on right now.

"I'm going to grab my laptop from my room. It's time to turn over every last stone we can find regarding Janie Simpson."

7

S team from the shower hung heavy in the air. Mia toweled off then found a warm sweater and leggings to slip into. The combination of the drizzling April temperatures and the current twist of events in her life refused to let the chill leave her bones.

Needing to put something more in her stomach than too many cups of coffee, she searched her refrigerator for potato soup she'd made over the weekend. Cooking usually soothed her, but right now, putting together a meal she probably wouldn't even be able to taste sounded far from appealing.

She grabbed the container with the soup, ladled a few scoops in a bowl, and zapped it in the microwave. Chet and Tucker's muffled voices rumbled through the wall, the sound comforting in the stillness of her apartment.

When the microwave beeped, she removed her lunch then settled onto the couch, tucking her feet under her with her bowl in the middle of her lap. Otto sat in front of her with wide eyes. "Sorry, boy. Not much I can offer you from this bowl."

The dog tilted his head, as if trying to decipher what she said.

She spooned a bite of creamy soup in her mouth and leaned back against the plush cushions. The buttery taste of the soup coated her tongue but dropped like lead down her throat. "You're not missing out," she told Otto.

Her phone vibrated in the side pocket of her leggings, and she fished it out. She frowned at the screen. Mom. She loved her mama, but their conversations had been strained since her break-up with Aaron. Her mama wanted her to move down to Florida to lick her wounds but dealing with the humidity was as low on her bucket list as listening to lectures from Mama about things Mia should have done differently to save her relationship. Not like anything she could have done would have stopped Aaron form being an asshole who was a thief and a cheat.

Knowing she couldn't put off the inevitable, and needing a distraction, she accepted the call and hit the speaker button. "Hey, Mama. How are you?"

"Oh, I'm just fine. Enjoying the sunshine. How's the weather in the mountains?"

"More rain today," Mia said, setting her bowl on the coffee table then patting the couch to invite Otto up beside her.

"You should come visit. I'd love to see you." The deep drawl made Mia smile.

Escaping the craziness of the graves and the slashed tires and murdered women might be the best thing she could do. But running away from her problems wouldn't solve them, and no amount of miles would erase Chet's sad eyes from her memory.

"I can't do that, Mama. I have a new job. Responsibilities. I can't just take off on a vacation now." Keeping details of her life from her mom made her cringe. Growing up with a single mom had made the two of them more like friends than mother and daughter. Secrets were never an issue with them, but Tracey would flip her lid if she found out what Mia had been through the last couple days. Which would result with her mom flying up to Tennessee, something Mia couldn't handle right now.

Tracey let out a long sigh. "Have you talked to Aaron at all?"

Her spine stiffened. "No. Nor do I plan to."

"What about your money? Your dreams? Everything you two built together? I'm sure what happened was a big misunderstanding."

"We've talked this to death, Mama. Aaron is gone. Left without a trace. I couldn't talk to him if I wanted to. He wiped out our account, ran off with another woman, and left me to pick up the pieces."

A familiar bite of resentment pushed against her chest. "Why would you want me to be with someone like that? Why don't you understand that he almost destroyed me?" She hated the hitch of emotion in her voice, but she was tired of being the only one to stand up for herself—hated needing to convince her own mother that she was worth more than what a man like Aaron could give her.

"No man can destroy you, my strong girl. I'm so sorry if you feel like I'm pushing you to go back to something—someone—who isn't good for you. Sometimes it's hard not to project my past onto you."

Although Mia appreciated the words, she couldn't quite believe them. This same circle of conversation had spun between them more times than she could count. If her mom really meant what she said, she'd stop bringing up Aaron and just support Mia's new life.

"It's fine, Mama." A yawn ripped through her. She plucked the fleece throw blanket from the back of the sofa and pooled it over her lap, causing Otto to grumble and move his head to her side. "Can I call you later? I didn't sleep well last night and want to close my eyes for a bit."

"Are you feeling all right?" Tracey asked, concern clear in her voice.

Mia fought a humorless laugh. A lot of feelings whirled around her, and none of them made her feel all right. "I'm fine. Just need a little nap. We'll talk later. Love you."

She disconnected the call then slid down on the couch, resting her head on the fuzzy throw pillow. The rumbles of conversation from next door continued, and she concentrated on Chet's deep baritone until her eyelids fell and she drifted into a deep sleep.

Grrrr! Ruff! Grrrr!

Otto's deep rumbles vibrated from his throat, yanking her from a dreamless sleep. He stood beside her, teeth bared and the hairs on the back of his neck standing straight up.

A charged energy sizzled in the air, and Mia straightened, adrenaline forcing away all traces of fatigue. Shadows fell across the floor. No light filtered through the windows, and she hadn't turned on any lamps before she'd fallen asleep. The sound of heavy raindrops pounded against the roof.

A quick glance at the glowing clock on her stove told she'd slept the afternoon away. Evening was here, and the sun must have just set. Otto kept guard beside her, his growls increasing her anxiety. She swiped her phone from the coffee table and stood.

She twisted the knob on the lamp beside her, the immediate glow chasing away the shadows. She glanced around the room. Nothing was out of place. No strangers lurked in the corners. Crossing the room, she checked the front door and released a breath of relief to find it still locked. She flipped on the kitchen light. Something outside the window caught her attention.

Illuminating the porch, she squinted and stared out the rectangular glass that flanked the door. Long strands of fabric or string dangled from a tree in the front yard. The wind blew, causing the strands to dance around. The strands were almost like unlit Christmas lights that had gotten loose and wiggled around on the branches. But Christmas lights hadn't lingered in the trees when she'd moved in January, so why would they be put up in April? And who would put them there in the middle of a rainstorm?

She squinted through the darkening sky. The strands were thicker than they first appeared, and nothing adorned the thick cords. The shapes took form, and her brain caught up to what her eyes saw. Someone didn't put strands of lights in the tree. Someone had tied ropes to the branches, letting them hang down like long snakes.

THE BRIGHT LIGHT glowing from Chet's computer strained his eyes. He'd stared at the screen far too long. His head ached and the muscles in his neck screamed at him to take a break. But his obsessive need to find out everything he could about Janie Simpson compelled him to keep reading. Keep digging.

The information he uncovered was mostly mundane, and probably already found by the police, but he couldn't just sit here and do nothing. So he sat and searched and prayed to find anything that would prove useful.

His phone rang, and Mia's name popped up. He answered the call and lifted the device to his ear. "Hello?"

"Chet! Come here! Now!"

Mia's frantic cries pitched his heart to his throat and had him running toward the door. "I'm coming." He threw open the door just as Mia flew out of her apartment. Her wide, worried eyes displayed her panic. Otto stood beside her, his body clenched and coiled as if ready to strike some unseen attacker any second.

"What's going on? Are you all right?"

She pointed behind her. "Someone tied ropes in the tree."

Her words made no sense, and he peered past her to the clutter of trees in the front yard. When Bobby had built this cabin years before, he'd wanted a simple hide away in the woods for hunting and fishing—two activities his wife wasn't a fan of. He'd cleared enough space to build the square home, make a narrow path for a driveway, and pour a small fishing pond in the backyard. He left the land as unspoiled as possible, and the wind from the ongoing storm made a handful of maple trees sway.

Through the haze of rain, he could make out what looked like thick snakes whipping from wayward branches in a tree that stood directly in front of the house, a smattering of pine trees around it. The wind howled, giving the illusion that the strands screamed as they danced around. Dark clouds moved across the moonless sky. "What the hell?"

"I fell asleep. Otto woke me. He was upset and put me on edge. When I checked around my place, I noticed something outside." Quivers of fear shook her voice. "I think it's rope."

"Go inside and lock the door. Call the police. Now."

She shook her head. "I'm scared. I don't want to be inside by myself."

Not wanting to waste time arguing, he said, "Fine. Stay close. But call the cops."

He pounded down the steps, the drizzle of rain spraying him, and marched straight to the tree. His heart raced. Sweat collected on the back of his neck and the scars on his wrists burned, as if he'd just burst from the ropes that once bound him. As he got closer, the thick, corded material became undeniable. A handful of separate strands of rope dangled from different heights, dancing in the wind. Mocking him.

"This is Mia Tulley. I need an officer out at my place immediately."

Mia might be close to his back, but she sounded so far away. Apprehension pressed down on his chest like a weight, stealing his breath. His lungs burned. Black dots flickered in his vision, giving the dangling ropes an animated quality as if they were flying at him. Coming for him.

"Someone was here," Mia continued. "They tied ropes in the tree. I...I think it might be some kind of a threat."

Chet crouched on the lawn, the ground squishing beneath his feet. The stars peeking through the shifting clouds blurred. His body swaying along with the physical reminders of the constraints that had once held him. Had kept him from saving his family.

Had kept his family from freeing themselves from the monster who'd stolen their lives.

A soft touch on his shoulder tensed his muscles.

"Police are on their way. Let's go inside." Mia spoke gently, as if trying to coax a shy child.

He couldn't move—his limbs frozen and gaze glued to the haunting scene before him.

"Whoever did this might still be out here. It's not safe," Mia said. She cupped her palm under his elbow to help him stand.

He leaned on her, accepting her assistance but making sure not to put too much weight on her tiny frame. She slid her arm around his back and led him to her apartment. He went willingly—numbly, unable to make sense of what was happening. Or why. He welcomed the blankness of his mind. The dark fuzz of nothing was better than all the questions with no answers.

"You're all wet. I'm going to grab a towel. You sit here with Otto." She steered him to a two person-table in the corner of her kitchen. He sat and hunched over, his forearms resting on his knees.

Mia returned with a thick, white towel and draped it over his shoulder. "Do you want some tea? It will warm us both up, and I need to keep my hands busy."

She rambled on, a trait of hers he'd come to enjoy as she grabbed a silver kettle from her stovetop and filled it with water before placing it on the flickering flames under the burner. Otto sat beside him, his head rested in his lap. Chet concentrated on the subtle hum of Mia's voice, the words not registering but not really mattering. He understood that she talked and prepared a warm drink he hadn't asked for to soothe her nerves as much as his.

So he let her speak, and the too-quick cadence of her gentle tone loosened something inside him. Melted his tension and released the mounting pressure in his chest until he could finally inhale a deep breath.

She set a dainty white cup with a tiny chip on the lip in front of him. "Milk or sugar?"

He shook his head, straightening to watch her fill her own teacup and bring it to the table.

"I should have known that." She offered him a timid smile that didn't quite reach her eyes. "You always drink your coffee black. Usually that's the same with tea."

"Thanks."

Silence weaved between them, but for once, it wasn't awkward or uncomfortable. But the unspoken questions were as loud as the heavy panting from Otto's open mouth.

Mia chewed her bottom lip, her hands wrapped around her cup. "Can I ask you a question?"

"Yes," he said on a heavy sigh. Just like before, he knew what she wanted to know and dreaded discussing it. But she was a part of whatever the hell was happening and deserved to know everything.

"Why ropes?"

Propping his elbows on the table, he exposed his wrists. "He knocked me out when I came home. When I woke, he'd bound my wrists and ankles with rope. And now he's back, using the same material that bit into my skin—that I still feel wrapped around my hands—to torture me in a completely different way."

8

The yellow crime scene tape weaving between the tree trunks in the front yard was like a shining beacon, announcing to anyone nearby that Mia's sense of security had been breached. She shut the gauzy curtains across the living room window, the taillights of Cruz's police car still visible through the thin material.

A chill swept over her. If she could see through the curtain, anyone out there could see her.

Forcing a note of positivity to her voice she didn't possess, she turned to Chet who made her couch look as if it belonged in a child's playhouse. "At least Beau got all the ropes down, even if they still marked the area as a crime scene." Not like it mattered. She'd never erase the image of the long ropes hanging from the branches in the silent, gray sky from her mind.

Chet rested his head on the back of the couch, his face lifted toward the ceiling. "Sure."

His one-word responses might have driven her crazy before, but now she understood Chet a little bit more. Heck, she couldn't even blame him for his surly demeanor. She wouldn't want to welcome each day, filling it with pointless chatter, after what he'd been through.

Wanting to comfort him, but not knowing what to say, she settled beside him on the couch. Otto laid at her feet, refusing to leave her side. She hooked up her knee, using her dangling foot to rub over Otto's back. Her mind spun. As much as she wanted to help Chet right now, she was freaking out. Her already messy life had taken a nosedive right into shitsville.

"Say it," Chet said, swiveling his head to face her.

She frowned. "Say what?"

"I can see your wheels spinning."

"You can?"

"I've spent enough time with you to know when something's on your mind. That little line on the bridge of your nose creases."

She lifted her finger and touched the spot between her brows. "It does?"

He widened his eyes, answering her in his favorite way —with no words.

She drew in a deep breath. She didn't want to make him uncomfortable, but he'd asked so she might as well unleash the flurry of activity brewing inside her. "Why would this guy slash my tires and tie ropes on the tree in our yard?" She'd asked Cruz the same question after she'd given her statement, but his answer rang more like a run-of-the-mill response used to placate her. Not a real answer. At least not one that made sense.

"I don't know. It feels like he's messing with me. Like I got away from him and he wants to make me pay for living."

As much as she hated the idea of some sadistic criminal playing mind games with Chet, she understood Chet's train of thought. "But why me? Do you think he saw me in the woods? Maybe he thinks I saw him, or something that could point to him. But if that was the case, I would have already told the police. Playing with my mind now wouldn't benefit him."

"How does any of this benefit him? What does he gain from killing women and branding their skin?"

"I guess I never thought of it like that. I've never really looked at things through the eyes of a killer." Goosebumps tingled the skin of her forearm, and she grabbed the blanket that had been tossed on the floor from her earlier nap. She wished she could hide under the warm, fleece throw and forget this day had ever happened.

"It's not a fun place to go." Chet wiped a palm over his face then let his hand drop to his side. "But the more we can make sense of him, the easier it will be to catch him."

"I bet you were a good cop," she said. It was funny how she'd seen him as a pain in the butt coworker since she met him. A giant of a man who liked to cook and bake and bark out orders. She'd been told he was an officer at one point, but she'd never been able to imagine him in a police uniform, patrolling the streets or helping others in need.

But that had changed. She could see not only the slivers of vulnerability that would help a policeman empathize with others but also the way his brain worked. The way he attacked a problem head on, searching for answers and looking at the situation from different angles.

Wanting to know more and sensing they both needed a distraction, she pressed. "Do you miss it?"

"Sometimes."

"Where did you learn to cook?" She'd been impressed by his skills in the kitchen, although she'd never told him so. He'd put up a huge, concrete wall between them the moment she stepped foot at the retreat. Breaking through was impossible before, and she'd quickly given up trying.

He shrugged. "Just picked it up."

She fought the urge to roll her eyes, even though a tickle of amusement leaked through the irritation of his refusal to give her a straight answer. "While working at the station? From your wife?"

He winced, a flash of pain deepening the brown of his eyes. "My mom worked nights. Dad wasn't around. My cousin lived with us. If we wanted to eat, I had to cook."

"I get that," she said, thinking back to her own childhood and nights spent alone while her mama picked up extra shifts at the diner. "But I just had to feed myself. No siblings. No cousins. Just me and my mama. Are you and your cousin still close?"

Another flash of pain contorted his features. "She died. About a year ago."

His admission smacked against her chest, and she fell further back into the couch. So much loss had to be hard to bear. "I'm sorry. Losing her after already losing your wife and daughter had to be difficult."

Shifting on the couch, he met her gaze with a long, heated stare. Indecision bounced in his pupils, as if he wasn't sure how much he wanted to confide.

She wouldn't press, wouldn't ask, but she hoped that if nothing else came from these last couple days, he'd learned he could trust her.

He blew out a long, shaky breath, refusing to break eye contact. "My cousin, Julia, worked in the kitchen with me at Crossroads Mountain Retreat. She'd just graduated college and put in a dozen applications for jobs across the state, all resulting in rejection. She came to work with me in order to figure out her next steps. But things didn't go as planned, and now she's gone. One more person I should have protected."

She had no words to offer, nothing to wipe away the misery threaded through his voice. So she sat and pet Otto while Chet stared into space. Neither one of them moved. Neither one of them spoke. She searched for something more to say, wanting him to stay longer. Needing the security he offered just by being near.

Chet rubbed his hands over his jeans and stood. "It's getting late."

Panic pushed her to her feet, and she stared up at him. "Please don't go. I don't think I can be alone tonight."

His jaw dropped and brows rose. He rubbed the back of his neck, and a hint of pink tinged his cheeks. "I... umm...well..."

Laughing, she slapped at his chest, shocked at the direction his mind took. But the heat from his chest and the feel of hard muscles had her yanking back her hand and averting her gaze. "I'm scared that whoever is doing this will come back."

Chet glanced down at the couch and cringed. "I can't sleep on this thing."

She wrung her hands, embarrassment flaming her face. Sleep would never happen tonight, but she wouldn't ask him to stay again. She had a little bit of pride left.

"My couch is pretty comfortable. Hell, I could even sleep on it if you'd want to take my room"

The idea of sleeping in his bed made the flames of humiliation burn into something much deeper, much stronger. Tiny flickers of desire wiggled in her belly, and she mentally stomped them out. Chet offering her to stay at his place for the night was a huge step. Chivalry at its best and nothing more. Not like she wanted more anyway. After her break-up with Aaron, any kind of relationship was the last thing on her mind. "Are you sure?"

A tiny smirk tipped the corner of his mouth. "Why not?"

"Fine, but I'll take the couch. Just give me a second to pack a bag." She rushed away to grab what she needed for the night, making a mental note to find her most unattractive pajamas.

CHET FLIPPED ON HIS SIDE, kicking away the sheets that had wrapped around his legs. Sleep never came easy, but last night had been torture. With his past colliding with this present, and Mia curled up on his couch, his eyelids had hardly stayed shut longer than twenty minutes.

It didn't matter. He was used to functioning on fumes. He'd been doing it for years. He'd learned long ago it was better to stumble out of bed blurry eyed and exhausted than toss and turn to no avail. At least this way he'd catch the sunrise.

Sitting on the edge of the bed, he stretched his arms above his head then padded over the plush carpet to his dresser. With Mia in the next room, stumbling to the kitchen in his boxers wasn't an option. He scooped a pair of worn jeans from the bottom drawer then buttoned a red and black flannel across his chest before heading toward the scent of fresh coffee.

The sight of Mia standing in his kitchen with tousled hair and heavy-lidded eyes made his steps falter and squeezed his heart. She rubbed her bare foot over her calf, her skin exposed with checkered shorts that were barely visible under a baggy T-Shirt. She rose on her toes and reached into a cabinet. There was something intimate about a woman in her sleep clothes making him coffee. Even if the reason for her being there was innocent.

The tiny bursts of excitement in his gut terrified the hell out of him. This was why he'd held her at arm's length since they'd met. Sure, some of it was misplaced anger and resentment at seeing someone else stepping into Julia's shoes. But the bigger part had been the way his body had responded to Mia. Feelings that had laid dormant for a long time. Feelings that he didn't deserve to have for Mia or anyone else.

Needing to stop acting like a creeper, he cleared his throat. "Morning."

Otto sprang to his feet and ran down the hall.

Mia jumped, then pressed a hand over her heart. "You scared me to death."

He fought to hide a smile. "How'd you sleep?"

Returning to the cabinet, she swiped two mugs and filled them each from the pot. "Okay. You?"

"Not great." Forcing his limbs to work, he grabbed one of the mugs, making sure to give Mia as wide a berth as possible. "Thanks for this."

She smiled over the rim of her mug. "It's the least I could do. I was going to dress and watch the sunrise, but I don't think it would be as magical with the crime scene tape staring at me."

He hadn't thought about that. Watching the sun climb above the mountains, casting an array of orange and pink hues across the sky, was his favorite part of the day. But Mia was right. Sitting on the porch with a reminder of last night practically smacking him in the face wouldn't have its normally soothing effect. "How about the back deck? Won't see the sun come up but the view's still nice."

Her foot raised to rub against her leg again. "You don't mind the company?"

"Nope. Come on Otto." He made his way to back door, surprised that what he said was true. Not wanting to give it any more thought, he stepped out into the brisk morning air. Otto trotted behind him, running for the stairs and onto a patch of grass to do his business.

Chet settled onto an Adirondack chair and placed his coffee on the thick arm. Condensation coated the white wood and crept into his clothes. Crickets chirped in the distance and the hum of a new morning buzzed around him. Thick fog rolled over the small pond, his boat bobbing in the water by the dock. Sparks of pink glowed through the dark clouds, pushing away the night sky.

The door behind him banged shut.

"Chair's wet," he said.

"Thanks for the heads up." Mia skipped the chair and approached the railing that encased the deck. She leaned forward with her mug in her hands, her forearms on the wood. "I don't come out here much. It's nice."

He lifted his mug. Streams of steam curled into the air and lifted the scent of French Roast to his nose. Taking a sip, he savored the bitter taste and the jolt of caffeine. "Yep."

She turned to face him just as the glow of yellow light broke through the swirl of dawn. "What do we do now? I don't think I'll feel safe until this guy's caught, but I can't just press pause on my life until then."

"Then don't." He didn't have a guidebook on how to handle the shit life dealt. All he knew was to just put one foot in front of the other, come what may.

Chuckling, she shook her head. "Care to elaborate?"

He took another sip then cradled the mug on his lap. "You up for working this morning?"

She twisted her mouth to the side, causing her button

nose to crinkle. "It's better than sitting around and waiting for the other shoe to drop."

"Agreed. I'll let Brooke know we'll be in to serve breakfast. We'll see where things stand—how we're feeling—then figure out the rest of the day."

She sagged against the railing. "I like that. Get through one chunk of the day at a time. Makes it a lot more manageable."

His phone buzzed, and he checked the screen. A text from Cruz waited for him. He opened the message. A zip of adrenaline combined with the caffeine and vanquished any lingering fatigue from his sleepless night.

"What is it?" Mia asked.

"Another victim's been identified. Looks like we know what we'll be doing after breakfast."

9

Hurrying to get ready, Mia swept her hair into a stubby ponytail and threw on the first thing she found in her cluttered closet. Her standard outfit of black leggings and oversized shirt—long sleeved to combat the chill that had been in the air when she'd taken her coffee on the deck with Chet.

As she dressed, she marveled at how far she and Chet had come. Days before, she'd assumed he was just a mean man who chose to be grumpy. Who kept everyone at arm's length, snapping and snarling because he didn't want to let anyone in. Even those he appeared to have a good relationship with—Zoe, Cruz, Brooke—were all recipients of his sharp tongue.

But now she understood why he sought solitude. She had even learned why he'd been so dismissive of her in the kitchen. It had nothing to do with her or her skills, but everything to do with the pain it caused to see someone else taking his cousin's place. Under all the layers of hostility laid a man with a broken heart—plain and simple.

And that man who'd given her such a hard time had

invited her into his home to make her feel safe. Even now, he waited in her living room to calm her worry over being alone. A gesture that meant more than he'd ever know.

Not wanting to make him wait longer than necessary, she rushed down the hall to find him packing up Otto's belongings. A punch of disappointment struck her as hard as a real blow. "I'll be sad to see him leave."

"I'm sure he's sad to go," Chet said, placing the now empty food dishes in a duffel bag. He surveyed the space, as if searching for anything he might have forgotten, and a flicker of curiosity sparked on his face.

She sighed, knowing exactly where his thoughts rested. "It's sparse in here, but I have everything I need." The day before she'd noted Chet's nice belongings that filled his home. All things someone in their early thirties should have accumulated by now. A sturdy table for a family to gather around, furniture that wasn't threadbare, comfortable rugs to warm up the space. The two apartments might be mirror images with their beamed ceilings, fireplaces, and stainless-steel appliances, but that's where the similarities ended.

Although lacking a lot of personal touches, Chet's place was an adult's apartment with adult things whereas hers appeared as though she were a broke college student living off the bare necessities.

He shrugged, as if he didn't understand what she was talking about, but he dropped his eyes to his shuffling feet. "Looks nice."

"You're a horrible liar." She slipped on her shoes and stuffed her keys and phone in her bag before slipping it over shoulder. "I told you my ex took everything from me."

He gaped. "You meant *everything*?"

She pressed her lips into a tight line and nodded.

He let out a low whistle. "Sounds like a real winner. Any idea where he went?"

"Nope, and I don't care. I'd rather start all over and never have to deal with him again. If I tracked him down and tried to get anything back, he'd find a way to make my life worse." It had taken a lot of tears and personal growth to reach that conclusion, but she firmly believed she was better off to just move on and leave her past behind her. Chalk it up to a lesson learned the hard way.

Besides, when she finally earned enough money to start her restaurant, she'd accomplish her dream all on her own. Without an ounce of help from her scumbag ex, who probably would have attempted to take all the credit.

"Glad you feel that way." Snagging the handles of the duffel, Chet opened the door, waiting for her to exit then locking up before heading toward his truck.

Gray skies loomed above. Thin clouds stretched out like wispy threads of cotton candy. A light breeze rustled the green leaves. The rain might have stopped sometime throughout the night, but the threat of another storm hovered overhead. The yellow tape still surrounded the vandalized area. The barrier, and what laid within, was like a violent brawl in the bar—something she should ignore but demanding her attention.

The sight was as much of a shock to her system this morning as it had been last night. The ropes might have been cut down, but the sight of them would forever mar the once peaceful view. Unexpected tears welled in her eyes. She'd found a refuge here, and now all sense of safety was gone.

Otto nuzzled against her side, nudging her hand with his nose.

"You okay?" Chet threw the duffel in the back of the truck and rested his elbow on the edge of the cab.

"I keep trying not to think about what's happening," she said. "But I can't hide from it, ya know? It's right in the front yard." She flicked her wrist toward the tree, her heart heavy.

An edge of something white was pressed against the green blades of grass. She squinted and leaned forward. "What's that?"

Chet stomped over to her. "What's what?"

Mia dodged under the yellow tape to get a closer look. She used the tip of her shoe to scrape off uprooted grass and specks of mud. She flipped the edge of the material over. "Looks like a photo."

Chet commanded Otto to stay then lifted the tape, ducking beneath it to stand beside her. His sharp inhalation of breath set her on edge, and he crouched low to the ground. He cupped his mouth with a shaky hand. The muscles in his neck went rigid.

Apprehension made her shiver. "What is it?"

"A picture of Laurie and Riley."

THE CRINKLED PICTURE of his wife and daughter stared up at Chet from the large table in the conference room. Not wanting to flake out on Brooke, he and Mia had put together a rushed breakfast after he'd bagged the photo and brought it with him to work. He'd called Cruz to let him know what he'd found, and Cruz had agreed to meet him at the lodge.

Now, Chet sat on the edge of leather desk chair with a bouncing knee he couldn't control. For the second day in a row, the smiling faces he loved so much looked up at him from moments captured on film. But unlike yesterday, he had no memories associated with this picture. With this moment. As if he wasn't there when someone snapped a camera, forever memorializing the scene before him. Of Laurie sitting on a wooden glider, smiling at Riley swinging high from the playset in their backyard.

He'd seen this scene a hundred times, could hear Riley's giggle and demands to be watched as she swung higher and higher. But this particular picture didn't register in his mind. He hadn't taken the photo. So who had?

Anger swirled inside him like a brewing storm. He couldn't take much more. Couldn't handle yet another punch in the gut.

Lincoln stood at the head of the table, the backdrop of the mountains dominating the window behind him. He'd pushed aside the chair, choosing to stand and gain a better view of all of Chet's notes strewn across the table. "You saved all of this for three years?" he asked, his thumb propped under his chin.

Chet didn't want to admit that although he hadn't been able to look through the file since the case had gone cold, he also couldn't part with everything he'd collected. "Yep."

"We have a lot of the same information on file at the station," Cruz said, sitting across from Chet. Concern crinkled his brow. "But not everything. You never told me you kept looking into all this."

"You never asked."

Cruz shot him an are-you-serious look.

"You'd make a damn good detective," Lincoln said. "Thorough as hell."

Unable to look at the picture for another second, Chet leaned back in his chair. "You would be too, but what do you think about this? Looks like it's been folded and unfolded a hundred times."

Lincoln slid the evidence bag containing the photo toward him. "You sure it's not yours?"

"Positive." He kept all images of his past life tucked away. As if having constant reminders of what he used to have around him would increase his pain. Even though he knew that wasn't the case. The smiling faces of Laurie and Riley just sharpened their memory, chiseled their features in his mind. And if he was being honest with himself, had brought a flood of good memories that had given him something to smile about.

"Could belong to whoever was there last night. Fell out of his pocket," Cruz said. "It was dark as hell, and Beau might have missed it."

Chet cringed at the idea that the person who killed his family carried their picture around with him. Obviously taking it out and putting it away numerous times to cause all the damage to the once-glossy paper. "Tell me about the victim you just identified."

Lincoln worked his jaw back and forth. "I meant what I said about you making a damn good detective, but you're not an officer anymore. There are things we can't share with you about this case."

Chet rolled his eyes. "Don't give me that bullshit. I can help. No need to waste time, because we both know I'll find out whatever I want to know one way or the other."

The door swung open, and Tucker marched in, plopping down on one of the chairs as if he'd been asked to join them. "Just talked to Mia. She filled me in on what you found."

A low rumble vibrated from Lincoln's chest. "What the hell? This isn't a community project here, boys. It's a police investigation. One that Cruz and I have the ability to handle."

Chet worked his tongue over his top row of teeth,

reigning in his temper. Snapping at Lincoln wouldn't help his cause. "Consider us consultants. Ones who know the case and have insight you need. Will know about connections that could help you find a killer faster. This isn't Nashville. You don't have the same support here."

Groaning, Lincoln shook his head. "Fine. I know Cruz is already filling you in. Might as well use it to my advantage." Grabbing a tablet from the table, he swiped his finger across the screen. "The woman we identified this morning is Bonnie Preen. Age forty-seven. Reported missing eight months ago from a hiking trail in Kentucky."

"The sonofabitch gets around," Chet said. "That goes across state lines. Will the FBI want to be involved?"

Tucker tensed. "Maybe."

Chet nodded. More help wasn't a bad thing but involving the FBI could be hard on Tucker. Tucker's experience with the FBI on the case that ended his career didn't bring good memories. The case landed him in the hospital, injured Otto, and killed his close friend.

"They have a lot of resources we don't have," Cruz said. "My experience with them is if we play nice, so will they."

Wanting to get back to Bonnie Preen, Chet asked, "Any connections between the new victims and the ones we've already found?"

"Not yet. But it's early. We need to establish a pattern— create a profile," Cruz said, standing and circling the table. "I want to read over all this. See if there's anything you caught that's not on my radar. That was missed from the notes at the station. Maybe that will give me a clear image of who we're dealing with."

Tucker cleared his throat, his stare distant and unreadable. "I might know someone who can help create a profile."

His suggestion tugged at Chet's heartstrings, and gratitude flowed through him. "You don't have to do that." Tucker was referencing Elizabeth. An ex-FBI profiler, and the widow of his old pal. "I appreciate the offer, but man..." He let his sentence run off, not wanting to expose Tucker's past, and damnit, not being able to refuse his offer with any real sincerity.

Leaning forward, Tucker clapped a hand on Chet's shoulder. "Whatever can help find this bastard. The least I can do is ask." He smiled, but the wounds of his past shined in his blue eyes. Not even Tucker's easy-going personality could camouflage the scars he kept buried.

Crossing his arms, Lincoln frowned. "Who are you talking about?"

"Elizabeth Gilmore," Tucker said. "She worked for the FBI for years, one of their top profilers, before walking away."

Lincoln raised his brows. "I know her. She's good. You really think you could get her to work with us on this?"

Tucker lifted on shoulder. "If I can track her down, she just might."

Chet wouldn't hold his breath. He knew the long history between Tucker and Elizabeth. Chet wasn't so sure Elizabeth would do any favors for Tucker. Even to help track down a serial killer.

10

Now that expectations had been met and notes looked through, the urge to act pushed Chet to his feet. Police investigations weren't all action and drama like depicted on television and in movies. Usually, it took lots of research and way too much talking to track down leads.

One thing he was more than happy to have left behind. He liked getting his hands dirty. Digging in and seeing the desired outcome emerge from his hard work. Being the head of a small kitchen might be far from the police work he once loved so much, but nothing satisfied him more than seeing the fruits of his labor.

Something that wasn't always the case when he had worked on the force.

"So what's the plan?" he asked. He might have a few ideas of what the next moves should be, but he didn't want to step on anyone's toes. He sensed Lincoln wasn't completely sold on letting him be a part of things, even if he said otherwise. Rocking the boat wasn't a good idea. Better to follow along for now.

"Cruz will keep looking for connections among the victims. Tucker, can you let him know if you get ahold of Elizabeth? He can coordinate with her if she agrees to help."

Nodding, Tucker rose. "Can do. I'll see if I can get her on the phone. I still have her number but that doesn't mean she'll answer."

"Thanks, man." Chet watched his friend leave the room before focusing on Lincoln.

"I'll send the photo to the lab for prints. So far, we've struck out on that end, but if this fell out of the guy's pocket, he might have slipped up and left some evidence on it." Lincoln shuffled Chet's work into a neat pile before shoving it back in the file. "I want to take a closer look at the ropes tied on your tree."

"You think you can trace them?" Chet asked. He'd been so thrown by the ominous threat swinging from the trees the night before, he'd never thought they could be used to find the killer. Rope could be bought anywhere.

"I'm gonna try," Lincoln said. "Figure I can head to the trading post. The guy who runs it might be able to give me some details. If we're lucky, someone messed up. Used material we can trace back to who bought it."

"Let me go with you. I've known Eddy since we were kids. I'm close to his uncle, who owned the store before him."

"Might be good for you to take him along," Cruz said. "You're still an outsider here. Having a local might help soften people toward you. You can come off as kind of an ass."

Lincoln threw a pen across the room at Cruz. "The only reason people might not like me is because I look like you."

The banter between the twin brothers usually amused Chet, but not now. Not with so much at stake and a shit ton to do. "Eddy's always wanted to be best buds with me. Anything I ask, he'll answer then elaborate more than I ever cared to know."

Lincoln dipped his chin. "All right."

"What about Mia's car?" He didn't mind giving her a ride to and from work, but she'd want her vehicle back as soon as possible.

"It'll be cleared for her to pick up later today," Cruz said. "No prints. No evidence left behind."

"I'll bring her down to get it. But I want to talk with Eddy first."

Frowning, Tucker came back in the room. "I got ahold of Elizabeth."

Chet fought with the need to spring into action and be there for his friend. A few minutes wouldn't hurt anything, so he stayed rooted to the burgundy carpet. "How'd it go?"

Tucker slunk down into a chair, his weight shifting the wheels backward. "Umm, okay I guess. She said she'd help."

A wave of appreciation washed over him, and a little bit of hope broke through his shield of pessimism. Things were finally going his way, the pieces falling into place. The case was reopened with new evidence and victims to pour over, and now two new members of the team with a ton of experience could shine a new light on things. "Thanks for reaching out," he said, emotion wedging in his throat.

Tucker shook his head, his lips pressed in a thin line. "I just need a minute. Then I can do whatever you guys need."

"I have to let Mia know I'm taking off," Chet said as he made his way toward the door. "She should be in the kitchen. Said she was going to get an early start on lunch and prep for dinner."

Three pairs of eyes stared at him, mouths agape.

"What?" he snapped, hating the interested looks aimed at him.

Tucker threw his palms in front of him as if warding off Chet's temper. "Nothing. Just wasn't aware you and Mia were friends. Never knew you to check in with her."

Chet clenched his jaw, weighing his words wisely. Something had shifted inside him, softened him toward Mia. His instant attraction to her had made him throw up a million walls, the unwanted feelings causing guilt and confusion. But after spending time with her, he realized he'd been unfair. He'd taken out his own shit on her, something she didn't deserve.

Something he needed to make up for.

But he didn't need to announce that to the room. "She's scared, can you blame her? I told her I'd stick close. But if she's here, she's safe. I just want to let her know I'll be gone for a little bit."

All three men continued to stare, eyebrows now hooked as if they didn't buy his bullshit.

"Knock it off. Lincoln, I'll meet you in the lobby in ten minutes." He stormed away without giving them another look. He didn't need to explain anything to them. Hell, he couldn't even understand the urge to watch over and protect Mia.

He was just being neighborly. Something he hadn't felt compelled to do for a while. He'd been stuck in limbo, nursing his wounds and just making it through the day. But now, if justice could finally be dealt, he might start living again. Might see a future that was more than just cooking food and brooding at home alone.

For the first time in a long time, he smiled, knowing that good days laid ahead of him again. And he couldn't help but wonder if he had Mia to thank for that.

∿

A LOW WHINE drew Mia's attention to Otto. He stood in the doorway, eyes round and pleading. Tail straight and unmoving. "I'm sorry, boy. I know you need to go out."

She'd spent the last hour pouring over preparations for the rest of the meals for the day. Planning carefully to allow for crossovers tomorrow. Roast beef for dinner that could be made into a stew in the morning. Roasted peppers that she'd chop up and throw in with the eggs for breakfast—if there were leftovers.

She'd always been a good cook but working at the retreat had taught her how to be a better planner. A lesson she'd take with her when she left.

Lifting the lid from the roaster, she inhaled the scents of garlic and savory beef. "Give me just one second and I'll take you outside."

Brooke waltzed into the kitchen, hauling bags filled with pantry staples. "You know he won't talk back, right? Trust me. I've tried for years to get Wyatt to answer me and nothing."

Mia chuckled. "Where is Wyatt?" Brooke's tan and cream-colored mutt usually followed her around while she worked, but he was nowhere to be found.

"Home. I ran into town and didn't want him pestering anyone while I was gone. After I put this stuff away, I'll grab him." Brooke plucked a gallon of milk from a canvas bag and put it in the fridge. "We have a guest coming in a couple days who is vegan, by the way. You and Chet will need to make sure we have enough options for him."

"Chet will love that," Mia said, her tone dry. She rushed over to help put the groceries where they belonged. Chet hated others dictating his actions. Even if it was a guest with dietary restrictions.

"You two have spent a lot of time together the last couple days. How's that going?"

Otto barked, then whined again.

Mia winced, grateful for the excuse to leave and not dive into Brooke's question. "Sorry. I'd love to stay and chat, but I really need to take Otto outside. Then I need to take him back to the kennel for Tucker."

"It was nice of Tucker to let Otto stay with you last night." Brooke scratched behind the dog's ears. "Why don't you grab what you need, and I'll give you a ride down to the kennel on my way home. That why you don't have to be alone."

Brooke's concern made her smile. "Thanks. I'd say you're silly to worry, but I'll take all the company I can get. I even slept on Chet's couch, so I wasn't alone all night. I don't think I would have slept a wink otherwise."

"You what?" Brooke's mouth fell open. She clung to the edge of the island, making a dramatic show of trying to keep herself upright. "Chet never lets people in his house. Well, besides Tucker, but it's not like he waits for an invitation. More like barges in whenever he feels like it."

She scooped up Otto's water dish, emptied the liquid down the drain, and stuffed it in the duffel Chet had left with the rest of Otto's things. Heat rushed down the back of Mia's neck. Even if some ridiculous part of her—a part she had no desire to take a closer look at—wouldn't mind if her slumber party at Chet's had other implications, her stay there had been completely innocent. "I was scared. He was nice. Not a big deal."

Not wanting to talk more about it, she led the way out of the kitchen, knowing Brooke and Otto would follow.

Brooke's hurried footsteps chased Mia down until she strolled beside her in the long corridor. "But Chet being nice to you is a big deal. Even given the circumstances. I mean, I know he's a big pile of marshmallowy goodness inside, which is why I put up with his shit, but he doesn't show that part of him to many people."

Pressing her lips together, she shrugged. Discussing the dynamics between her and Chet didn't feel right, so she just wouldn't say anything at all.

When they turned into the lobby, Brooke waved at a man sitting in one of two couches around the large fireplace. Mia kept her head down. She didn't often mingle with the guests beyond the dining room, and even then it was to see if anything was needed. She'd worked at the retreat for months, but she hadn't ventured beyond the kitchen and the kennel. Feeling like too much of an outsider to use any other facilities—no matter how often Brooke insisted all the amenities were available to guests and staff.

A young woman not much older than Mia sat behind the front desk, and Mia offered her a smile before pushing out of the large wooden doors into the cool breeze outside. The sun was high in the sky, though shielded behind a thin layer of gray clouds. Brooke's baby blue golf cart was parked in the front of the lot—a color chosen by Lincoln after he'd moved in with Brooke.

"Did I upset you?" Brooke asked as she climbed behind the wheel.

Mia waited for Otto to jump on the seat beside Brooke before sliding on the vinyl bench with the duffel bag on her lap. "Sorry. I just have a lot on my mind." Her answer wasn't untrue if a bit evasive.

Brooke steered the cart onto the gravel path that led to the back of the lodge. "Trust me. I understand."

The towering lodge with its three stories of rounded logs disappeared and gave way to a large lake with blue water that rippled with the swirling air. An expanse of trees started at the edge of the trail carved along the lake and fanned out as far as the eye could see, the farthest tips reaching up to touch the skyline. Identical cabins were dotted along the lake with plenty of space between to give each guest—and Brooke—all the privacy they could want.

The kennel that housed the therapy dogs sat behind the lodge, on a patch of land in front of the lake. The small building was painted a burgundy red. A fenced-in section provided an area for the dogs to play. Although most of their exercise came from walking the trails and spending time with guests.

Brooke came to a stop in front of the kennel. "Want help taking Otto in?"

"I think I can handle it. I want to talk to Tucker and maybe spend some time with the dogs while I'm here." She climbed down then called for Otto. "Thanks for the ride."

Brooke gave a little wave then drove away, the cart bouncing down the incline to the trail.

Mia sighed, watching her go. Brooke had accomplished so much, and she was the same age as Mia. At thirty, she'd opened a successful business and was in a loving and stable relationship. Two things that seemed so far from Mia's reach.

Not wanting to get sucked into the gloom making ridiculous comparisons could create, she opened the door to the kennel and was greeted by a dangling bell overhead and barking dogs. A half door separated the front of the room from the dog-lined aisle, keeping the dogs hidden from view. "It's just me, everyone. Coming to say hello."

Otto preceded her inside, tail wagging and bouncing in

front of the miniature door then swinging it open with his
nose.

Mia laughed and followed him into the aisle that housed
the dogs. Each dog sat behind wrought iron gates that kept
them pinned in their little homes, a welcome mat at their
thresholds. A bed and a dish full of water were located in
each section, the food doled out on a strict schedule.
"Tucker?"

Nothing but the sounds of heavy doggy pants and the
clicking of nails on the tiled floor greeted her. Four dogs sat
in front of their doors, each one begging with their eyes to
be let out.

She secured Otto in his luxury cage then stepped further
down the aisle, peeking into an open door that stored dog
food and training tools Tucker used for the dogs. Extra
leashes hung from hooks and bins of toys and bones lined a
wire rack in the corner.

The sound of the bell chiming from the front rang in her
ears. Tucker must have stepped out for a second and
returned. Barking and low growls came from the kennels.
What was wrong with the dogs? Maybe a guest from the
retreat had wandered in, not realizing they needed Tucker
to assist with the animals.

Stepping out of the storeroom, she pivoted toward the
front door.

A man stood on the other side of the half-door. A black
ski mask over his face, a hoodie pulled over the top of his
head. The disguise unable to hide the cruel snarl on his lips.
"Nice to see you again. Mia."

11

The overhead light bounced off the gleaming marble countertops in the empty kitchen at the retreat. Not one dish was out of place, and the lemony scent of the cleaner Mia always used hung heavy in the air. She finished her work but left no clue as to where she'd gone.

Chet dug in his pocket for his phone and called her. Frustration had him muttering under her breath as the line rang and rang before landing in her voicemail. He punched the end button, choosing to send out a text then crushed the device in his hand.

Shutting off the lights, he stomped from the room. He didn't want to make Lincoln wait but couldn't leave without letting Mia know where he was going—making sure she was all right. A tingle of guilt tightened his gut. He didn't have the slightest clue where Mia would have gone. He'd worked alongside her for months now, lived right next door, and he hadn't learned enough about her to even guess where she'd spend her time outside of the kitchen.

Otto.

She'd said she'd take Otto back to the kennel when she got the chance. Calling her again, he bounded back up the three flights of stairs to the conference room. Tucker sat in the same spot, chair facing the window, a faraway look in his eyes, as if he was seeing something in front of him that wasn't really there. The phone went to voicemail, and he swore.

Tucker blinked and ran a palm over his face before shifting his focus to Chet. "I thought you were leaving."

"Mia's not in the kitchen. I thought maybe she contacted you about Otto." He pounded out another text as he spoke, for once wishing he had one of those newer phones. He didn't send many text messages. It took way too long on his phone, but parting with it had never been a thought.

Until now. When his thick fingers fumbled over the keys, having to click the damn buttons multiple times to get to the right letter.

"Shit. She was going to bring him by and help me out for a little while. Said it would take her mind off things." Tucker glanced at the wall clock and cringed. "I zoned out. I didn't realize how long I'd been up here."

"Check your phone. See if she called."

Tucker tilted up his phone that was laying on the table. "Nothing. But that doesn't mean she didn't head down there on her own."

"I'm going to check." Chet narrowed his gaze, searching Tucker's face. "You look a little pale, man. You okay?"

"Yeah. Fine. Go find Mia." He made the shooing motion with his hand then settled his stare back out the window.

A beat of hesitation slowed Chet's retreat, but there were bigger things happening than shooting the shit with Tucker. Besides, if his friend wanted to chat, he'd open his mouth and say something. Tucker wasn't one to hold back on anything, and if he wanted Chet around, he'd ask him to stay.

Decision made, he hurried back down the stairs and out the door—bypassing the fleet of golf carts. He jogged around the side of the lodge, and the sound of barking dogs raised the hairs on the back of his neck. The dogs were the most well-trained mutts he'd ever met, only barking when necessary.

Something wasn't right.

Pushing his stride longer, faster, he ran toward the kennel. The frenzied dogs were louder, more frantic as he approached. The door to the building stood ajar. He came to a stop, breaths tearing from his raw throat, and burst inside.

A man stood in the aisle, covered in black with a ski mask over his head, blocking Mia's exit. Dogs jumped on two legs, lunging at the doors keeping them caged. They barred their teeth and snarled, pissed they couldn't break through the barriers to get to the intruder.

Mia's eyes widened when he filled the doorway, and the man shifted to keep them both in view. With a knife in his hand, he lunged toward Mia, hooking one arm around her throat and jamming the tip of his knife against her side. "Don't do anything stupid."

Tears welled in Mia's eyes.

Fear pinched Chet's chest. He raised his palms, letting the man know he wasn't a threat—or at least pretending. The only way this asshole would get Mia out of this building was over his dead body. "No way you'll make it off the property with Mia. You might as well let her go and leave."

"You must think I'm an idiot," the man said, his voice muffled by the mask over his face and the constant sound of barking. "I'm taking her with me, and you're going to let me.

You don't want to be the reason another innocent woman dies, do you?"

The words slammed against him like a sucker punch to the gut, stealing his breath. Anger—and guilt—heated his veins.

Mia tightened her jaw, hands fisted at her sides. A flash of defiance sparked in her eyes.

His mind screamed to shake his head no. Reading Mia came so damn easily to him, and she was about to act. To do something that could get her killed. But if he told her not to move, not to put to action whatever plan was in her head, the man who held her by knifepoint might do something far worse.

Chet took a step backward. "You and I both know I won't let you walk away with her. Just put down the knife and step away from Mia."

The man laughed, hard and brittle. "Do you think I'm an idiot?"

Without warning, Mia lunged to the gate of the kennel that housed a snarling Otto. Her fingers lifted the handle, but not enough to open the door.

Her attacker grabbed a handful of hair and yanked her toward him. "You dumb bitch. I'm going to enjoy making you pay for that."

Chet tensed and watched Otto, willing him to bust free.

Otto threw himself against the barrier, snapping his jaw. The door flew open. Otto leapt into the air, sinking his teeth into the man's leg.

Mia's assailant flailed, releasing her as he kicked out his leg.

Chet stormed forward. He pushed through the half-door just as the man sprang loose from Otto's death grip. He kicked Otto's side, sending him into the metal grate of the cage. He faced Chet, knife in hand, and charged. He held the blade high as he ran, swiping downward.

Chet pivoted, but not before the sharp edge swiped down the side of his torso. A burning pain erupted, and he dropped to the ground. Blood coated his shirt, and a hiss of pain blew through his mouth.

The man fled out the door.

Mia collapsed on the ground beside him. "Oh my God! You're hurt. He stabbed you."

"Call the police," he said through clenched teeth. "They need to go after him."

Mia shifted him so he laid on his back then peeled his shirt from his torso. A deep gash sliced from the side of his waist down to his hip. "You need an ambulance. Now."

The dogs barked and howled. Desperate to be let loose to give chase.

Mia clasped a hand over his wound and applied pressure while she called 911.

Whining, Otto limped over and laid on the floor, resting his head on Chet's lap.

Chet closed his eyes, focusing on the heat of Mia's skin on his. The touch of her soft fingers. The sound of her voice. And tried to force out the loud voice inside him yelling that he'd almost been too late to keep woman under his protection safe. Again.

BLOOD COATED MIA'S HANDS. Terror shook her body. She had no idea how to help him, how to stop more blood from flowing from the knife wound on his side. All she could do was stay calm while keeping pressure on his wound and waiting for paramedics to come.

The dogs barked, not understanding the danger was gone. Otto stayed glued to Chet's side.

Chet propped himself up to a sitting position and leaned against the wall. He winced, his pain evident on the twisted lines of his face. "Stop fretting. I'm fine."

She choked out a pinched laugh over the ball of emotion clogging her throat. "Are you kidding me? You were stabbed. There's blood everywhere."

Brooke stormed inside, her brown hair swirling around her face and a gun trained in her steady hands.

"Chet's hurt," Mia yelled up at her. "Ambulance is on the way."

Chet's growl combined with the flurry of anxious dogs. "Go after him, Brooke. Call Lincoln and tell him to search the woods. Release the damn dogs. Do whatever you have to. Don't let that bastard leave this property."

"For fuck's sake, Chet." Brooke rushed inside and dropped to her knees. "I can't just leave and let you bleed out. I remember enough of my training. Let me take a look while we wait for the EMT's. You've lost a lot of blood. We shouldn't wait longer than necessary to try and stop you from losing more."

"Finally, someone with some sense," Mia said. She scooted to the side, calling Otto to her, allowing Brooke the space she needed to look over Chet, surprised when Chet tightened his grip on her hand to keep her from going too far.

Brooke slowly lifted Chet's shirt up his torso. "Looks like capillary bleeding. You're lucky. Mia, help him take his shirt off while I wash my hands. And Chet, lay down. You should know better."

Chet grumbled, as he yanked up his shirt. "Which is it? Take off my shirt or lay down?"

Brooke rolled her eyes and rushed away. "Down. Quiet. Stay," Her tone was hard as she barked out commands to the dogs, who all went quiet.

"Here. Let me help." Mia shooed away his hands. She unbuttoned his flannel then slid it off his shoulders. Blood rushed to her ears and heated her face. His hard muscles burned the tips of her fingers. She swallowed hard, pushing down the stupid reaction her body had to being so damn close to him. He was bleeding, and she'd barely escaped the clutches of a killer, her heart shouldn't be galloping in her chest because she was about to see him without a shirt on.

With the flannel off, she gripped the hem of the gray T-shirt he wore underneath. Her knuckles grazed against his abdomen, and he sucked in a sharp breath. "I'm sorry. Does that hurt?"

His eyes locked on hers, his pupils dilated. "No."

Her mouth went dry. She inched up his shirt, trying hard to keep the fabric from touching his wound. Trying to keep from touching the hard muscles of his stomach. She held his gaze. Intimacy wove a magic spell between them, erasing all other thoughts from her mind.

Brooke pushed through the door, breaking the moment. "Okay, I grabbed some things from the back."

Licking her lips, Mia dropped her gaze and backed away.

"You don't follow directions well." Brooke clicked her tongue then peeled the shirt the rest of the way off and threw it on the ground.

Mia's jaw dropped for a second before she snapped it closed. Not one ounce of fat could be found on Chet's chest and stomach. Chiseled muscle and defined abs dominated his torso. She fought not to use her hand to fan herself.

"This might hurt." Brooke took a damp cloth and dabbed at the open flesh.

Chet's hiss of pain moved Mia right back to his side. She linked her fingers in his and set their joined hands on her lap. "Almost done. You're okay." She didn't know if either of those statements were true, but if the only thing she could do to help was comfort Chet, she'd say whatever she could to ease his pain.

"The wound isn't too deep. The bleeding has pretty much stopped, but I want to apply some pressure just to be safe." Brooke took a long strip of white gauze and laid it against his wound, then pressed both hands against Chet's side.

"Sonofabitch." Squirming, Chet squeezed Mia's hand.

"Sorry," Brooke said, cringing. "Tell me what happened."

Mia blinked, focusing on the most terrifying moment of her life. "Umm, I brought Otto inside and Tucker wasn't here. I went in the back to see if he was in the storage room. The bell above the door chimed, and when I came back out a man was standing there."

"I'm sorry I just left you," Brooke said, her eyes round with remorse. "I should have stayed. Should have waited and made sure Tucker was here."

"It's not your fault," Mia said. "Chet came. He saved me. If he hadn't showed up, I don't know what would have happened."

Chet pinched together his lips. "I didn't do anything. You saved yourself."

Brooke tilted her head. "What did you do?"

"When Chet distracted the guy, I opened Otto's kennel. He bit the guy's leg. Then Chet charged."

Admiration shone from Brooke's eyes. "Smart thinking." She glanced at Otto and smiled. "Good boy."

"I tried to stop him when he ran out," Chet said, hanging his head. "He got by me. Now he's still out there. I missed my chance to stop him. To put an end to all of this."

The disappointment in his voice tugged at Mia's heart strings. "You don't know that. He might be in custody right now."

"I failed you, Mia," Chet whispered. "I'm sorry."

Mia ducked her chin and pushed into his sight line, forcing him to really see her. "You saved me. If you hadn't distracted him, he would have hauled me out of here. Would have killed me. You saved my life."

The sound of footsteps pounded toward them, and Tucker swung inside, his face red and heavy breaths panting from his mouth. "Paramedics are here. You okay, man? Mia?"

Otto jumped to his feet and walked to Tucker with his drooping tail wagging.

"He might need some stitches, but he'll be fine." Brooke continued applying pressure to the wound as she spoke.

"I don't need stitches."

Mia shook her head. "You need whatever the para-medics say you need so don't be a stubborn ass."

Her no-nonsense-tone gained a small smile from Chet. "Yes, ma'am."

A middle-aged woman with her blonde hair pulled into a short ponytail ran inside. "All right, Chet. Let's see what we're working with."

Brooke waited until the EMT dropped to a crouch beside her before moving out of the way. She placed a hand on Mia's shoulder. "Give her some space to look him over."

She didn't want to let go of Chet's hand—to sever their connection—but Brooke was right. The professional needed to do her job. "Be nice," she told him, then let Brooke help her to her feet. Tucker came to stand on her other side, her two new friends flanking her. She crossed her arms over her middle, willing her trembling legs to keep her upright.

Adrenaline leaked from her system, and she fought against the building tears. Now was the time to make sure Chet was taken care of. He didn't need to see her fall apart, to show her fear. To show him how much seeing him hurt affected her. That was something she'd unpack later, when she was alone and could really figure out what it meant. Because right now, the only thing she knew, was that seeing Chet bleeding on the ground gutted her in a way she'd never experienced and hoped to hell she'd never experience again.

12

With his eyes closed, Chet leaned his head on the back of the couch and gritted his teeth, wondering which he wanted more—the pain from his wound to subside or the crowd of people to get the hell out of his house.

Okay, crowd might be a bit of an overstatement, but until a few days ago, having more than one other person in his home was enough to make his skin itch. Now, Mia banged around in the kitchen, convinced he needed something to eat. Brooke and Lincoln sat at his table, discussing the search through her property that resulted with no sign of the man who'd held Mia at knifepoint, and Tucker hunched over in the recliner beside him.

All he wanted was to be alone and lick his wounds. Failure sat heavy on his chest. He should be on the hunt with Cruz, but exhaustion and the severe ache from his injury kept him on the sidelines. The doctor from the emergency room insisted he rest and keep an eye on the seven stitches trailing up his body. The earlier events played on repeat in this mind, each time beating into his head how he'd messed up again. How he hadn't gotten his hands around that bastard's scrawny neck.

He'd felt so helpless when Mia was held hostage and he couldn't do a damn thing about it. He'd promised himself he'd never be in that situation again. Never be at the mercy of someone else or let someone he cared about be threatened or harmed. Yet here he was.

Then there was Mia. He'd done everything he could do to keep her away and stop the feelings that snuck up on him from growing. But he hadn't stopped a damn thing. He couldn't deny his attraction to her from the start, but now his emotions were deeper—his feelings stronger than he wanted to admit to anyone. Especially himself.

"Grilled cheese and tomato soup." Mia's voice chirped beside him.

The smell of salty cheese and basil prompted him to open his eyes. Mia hovered over him, her brows knit with concern. He managed a small smile for her benefit, although the last thing he wanted was food.

"I'm not moving until you take a bite."

Sighing, he lifted a spoon full of red soup to his mouth. Surprised by the rich, full flavor, he took another sip. "Did you make this?"

A triumphant smirk played on her lips. "Yes. Maybe you need to loosen the reins at work a little, huh?"

He shrugged, then slurped more soup before taking a bite from the warm sandwich. Damn, she was a much better cook than he realized. He'd been so hellbent on keeping her away that he'd never given her a fair shake. Lesson learned.

The front door swung open. Wade McKenzie, the local bar owner, stomped inside with full white, plastic bags dangling from his fingers. "Brought your favs, buddy. How ya feeling?"

Chet bit back a groan. His friends meant well, but things were getting out of hand. "I'm fine." He bit out the words after swallowing another mouthful of creamy cheese and toasted bread.

The gruff tone didn't ruffle Wade's feathers. He dipped his chin in greeting to everyone around the room then hefted the crinkling bags on the counter. "I see you already have something to eat, so I'll put this in the fridge. It's not even Sunday, and I made ya some fried chicken."

Wade's fried chicken was famous in the area, and he only cooked it on Sunday nights at the Chill N' Grill.

"Something smells good," Wade said, either oblivious to Chet's irritation at another visitor or not caring. "Got enough for another bowl?" He shot Mia a wink, the dimples deepening in his cheeks.

Chet tensed, not liking the way Mia shook her head in amusement and grinned at Wade's flirty manner. "This isn't a damn party. Why are you all here?"

Mia hurried into the kitchen and spooned soup into a bowl then handed it to Wade. "Everyone's concerned."

"They should be," he snapped. "But not with me. I'm fine. Everyone should be out there. Finding this guy." He tossed down his spoon then flicked his wrist toward the front window.

"We're regrouping," Lincoln said. "We know more about the suspect now than we did before and need to take that into account. We have a good estimate of his height and weight, and Mia noticed a slight smokey smell to his clothes. These are all things to consider."

"Agreed," Chet said. "But now that they've been considered, it's time to move. What about Eddy? Weren't we going to speak with him?"

"*We* aren't doing anything." Lincoln stood. "I'm headed to the hardware store now."

Chet jumped to his feet, the sudden motion making him a little dizzy. "Eddy will talk to me. I want to be there."

"I'm asking him about rope. Not interrogating him. I think I'll be fine."

Bracing himself with a hand on the back of the couch, he faced off with Lincoln. He wouldn't stand for being pushed aside. "Now wait a minute."

"How about I go with him?" Tucker said. "Eddy will talk to me as much as you. No need for us both to be there. You stay here and relax."

"I don't need to relax. I'm—"

"Yes, we know. You're fine," Mia said. "The stitches up your side might say differently."

He raised his eyes to the ceiling. "Stitches are nothing. I'm not on bed rest or under doctor's orders."

"No," Brooke cut in. "You're under our orders to stay put. You and Mia both need to take some time off. Stick together until this is over. You going with Lincoln leaves her vulnerable."

Mia stiffened but didn't argue.

Chet's indignation deflated like a punctured balloon. Brooke was right. Leaving Mia's side wasn't something he could do.

"I could always stay with Mia," Wade said as he shoveled spoonfuls of soup in his mouth. "She can give me her recipe for this tomato soup so I can put it on my menu."

A light blush stained her cheeks. "You really mean it?"

"Absolutely."

"You can't have her recipe," Chet all but growled. "She needs it for her own place one day. And she doesn't need you to stay. Eat your soup and get back to work. She'll stay here with me."

Mia hooked up one eyebrow.

"I mean, if she's okay with that," he stammered. What the hell was that? Jealously over her reaction to Wade's praise had made him demand what he had no right to demand, but damnit, he couldn't just stand by and watch her bond with the biggest player in town.

Tucker burst out laughing, while Lincoln snorted then slid on his shoes. Brooke hid a grin.

Chet sighed. He'd just made a fool of himself. This was why he didn't like people invading his personal space. He was tired and cranky and so on edge he was about to fall over the brink of sanity.

"I'd like to stay," Mia said. "You might be fine, but I'm pretty shaken still." She turned her back to the room and busied herself making another grilled cheese on the griddle.

Wade slurped down the rest of his soup. "Let me know if you change your mind about the recipe. And anytime you want to talk about a restaurant of your own, I've got two good ears and lots of experience. Have Chet bring you down to the restaurant." He shot Chet a bemused look, then raised a hand in a wave. "See ya'll later. Let me know if there's anything I can do. Shoot me over what you know about this guy. I'll keep my eyes peeled."

"I'm off too," Brooke said, joining a hand with Lincoln's. "You two take the rest of the day off. Mia already prepped everything. Zoe and I can serve."

Chet watched as everyone filed out. A part of him longed to go with them. To pound the pavement and turn every stone in town until he found the man who'd threatened Mia. The other part, the part that grew with every second, was happy to finally be alone with Mia.

Now he just needed to figure out what the hell he wanted to do about it.

TWENTY MINUTES LATER, Mia scoured Chet's stovetop so hard her wrist hurt. All the dried food from the meal she'd made earlier was long gone, but she kept scrubbing—kept cleaning. Her nerves were so tight they threatened to break through her skin. Her mind raced as if she'd poured a gallon of coffee down her throat. No matter how busy she'd kept herself, she couldn't erase the image of the masked man with the knife from her head.

Her heart slammed against her breastbone. She heaved in deep, shaking breaths then blew them out her mouth.

"Are you okay?"

She jumped at the sudden sound of Chet's voice and slapped a hand over her chest. "You scared the crap out of me. I thought you were asleep."

Rocking back on his heels, he ran his fingers through his beard. "Sorry. Just woke up." He roamed his gaze over the kitchen. "I think it's clean. I mean, the punch of disinfectant is giving me a headache."

Mia winced. Maybe the fumes were getting to her. That's why her body was trembling, and a dull throb pulsed in her head. "Sorry. I just need to keep my hands busy."

"Or what?"

The well of tears she'd fought all day broke free. Her face crumpled, and she lifted her hands in a desperate display of giving up. "Or this."

Chet scratched the back of his neck. "Sorry. You wanna clean the bathroom?"

A laugh burst through her sob. "No thanks."

A sheepish grin appeared on Chet's face. "I'm bad at this stuff." He squirmed, his discomfort more evident than the cloud of lemon spray that hung in the air.

"You're better than you think." She rubbed her toe against the hardwood floors. "I'm just overwhelmed. Feeling a little panicky knowing some guy who wanted to kill me is still out there. Lurking somewhere. I can't stop thinking about it, and it's making me crazy."

"I understand."

She tilted her head to the side, studying his wounded eyes. "You do?"

He nodded. "After Laurie and Riley were killed, I started having panic attacks. I still have PTSD. It's been a long, painful road."

Needing to comfort him in some small way, she placed her palm on his arm. "I can't even imagine how you've dealt with everything you've lost. What helped you get through?"

He dropped his gaze to her hand and smiled. "This place. Friends forcing themselves into my house to check on me."

She chuckled. "I got a glimpse of that today."

"Then there was figuring out how to quiet my mind. That was the hardest part."

"What did you do? I mean, I'd take any advice right now to get my mind to shut up for a minute." She moved her fingers along his skin. The hairs of his arm brushing against her.

"Do you really want me to show you?"

She nodded.

He dipped his head toward the back door. "Grab your shoes."

Slipping on her sneakers, she met him at the back door then followed him onto the deck. She inhaled the fresh air.

The sun peeked through the clouds, warming the day and chasing away the threat of more rain. After her morning coffee with the view of the pond and the surrounding trees, she'd told herself she'd enjoy this more, but hadn't thought it'd be today.

But this time, Chet didn't settle onto a chair. He bounded down the stairs onto the lawn and hurried to a small shed she'd never seen the inside of.

She waited for him to emerge with two fishing poles, one in each hand, and a slow smile on his handsome face. Not convinced this was the right move, she scrunched her nose. "Fishing?"

His smile morphed into a shit-eating-grin, and she could almost see the little boy he used to be. Ornery and carefree. Just wanting to be outside, getting his hands dirty and driving his mom a little bit crazy. "Ever been?"

She shook her head, and the curls of her hair bounced around her face. She hooked a strand behind her ear and mustered as much enthusiasm as she could. Chet sharing a pastime with her was a big step. She didn't want to make him feel as though she didn't appreciate it. Besides, what could it hurt? "My mom wasn't much of an outdoorswoman. We did mostly inside activities, when she had time do anything beyond work."

"Same, but Julia and I always played outside. Always got into trouble. Fishing was one of our favorite things to do." Sadness skittered across his expression. He turned to look at the pond. "Having my own place to come down and fish whenever I wanted was one of the reasons I rented this place. That and knowing I'd have my privacy." He faced her again with raised brows and a smirk.

She laughed. "Looks like that flew out the window. Sorry about that. I didn't realize a hermit lived next door when I moved in. I just saw a nice, clean apartment available at a hell of a deal."

"Bobby has a good heart. Always has. I'm sure he's not charging either of us half of what he should."

His statement sobered her. "Do you really think so? I don't want to take advantage of anyone." She understood all too well what it was like to be on the losing side of that kind of arrangement.

"People round here look out for one another," Chet said. "Especially Bobby. He does what he can to help anyone in this town. You should feel like one of us now. Hell, even with his hardware store. He would have worked there forever if it wasn't for Eddy."

Mia grabbed one of the poles from Chet and walked beside him to the dock. The warm rays on her skin relaxed her. The sound of the birds chirping calmed her tangle of nerves. Maybe this exercise was more about being in nature than the actual fishing, which was fine by her. "What do you mean?"

"Eddy didn't have the best home life. His dad roughed him up then his mom would send him to Bobby and Missy's place. Bobby treated him like the son he never had, and when Eddy had trouble finding a job, he pretty much handed over the store."

Finding a place to sit on the old dock, Mia settled on her bottom and tucked her feet under her. "That's so nice."

"That's Bobby, and most folks in Pine Valley. It's a good place to live. Most the time." A dark cloud seemed to appear over his head as he stared out into the water then cast his line.

"Aren't you supposed to put a worm on the hook first?" Mia asked, not wanting to venture into more somber conversation.

"Says the woman sitting on her ass with her pole on the ground." Amusement laced through his words, but he kept his focus on the white and red bobber dancing on the surface of the water.

"Fair point."

Chet waited a few minutes then reeled in his line again. His phone rang, and he shifted to pull the device from his pocket and checked the screen.

This time, she laughed at his old school phone. "Why do you still have that thing? No one uses a flip phone anymore."

All traces of humor fled, and Chet's shoulders dropped. "It's the only way I can still hear the voices of my wife and daughter."

13

C het focused on the slight breeze against his face. He kept his gaze on the ripple of waves expanding along the surface of the lake. He cast his line, his admission sitting heavy in the air between him and Mia. He'd never admitted to anyone why he kept the stupid, old phone. With its cracked screen and tiny keys. He'd never told a soul that when he was at his lowest and needed something to remind him of better days, he'd listen to old voicemails his wife had left—his daughter giggling or hollering in the background.

Old videos were too painful, pictures shredded his heart, but listening to their voices was like a healing balm over the wounds that would never go away.

But when Tucker's name popped up on his screen, he didn't have time to dive into any of that with Mia. With his fishing pole in one hand, he flipped open his phone and pressed it to his ear. "Hey. What's up?"

"We spoke with Eddy. Turns out the rope used on the trees isn't super common."

Chet straightened. "Who sells it?"

Mia narrowed her gaze and rose to her feet, the fishing pole forgotten on the dock.

He couldn't answer her unspoken questions right now.

"Eddy sells it, as well as a couple other stores that specialize in wilderness and hunting gear. The company who manufactures the material is close by, and mostly distributes to the surrounding area. He remembers selling that specific type of rope a few weeks ago and handed over his security feed for us to review. He says he'll keep his eye out for anyone else buying it and let us know right away."

The news rocked Chet. "Are the other places Eddy knew of close?"

"A couple counties over. Plus there's online purchases."

"Could this mean this guy is from the area?" The idea shook the very foundation that kept him upright. This town, and the people in it, had rallied around him when his worst nightmare became his reality. People showed up—whether he wanted them to or not—and made sure he came out the other side alive. To think that someone among them was the one who'd brought this into his life...into the lives of every one of those victims they'd uncovered...was unimaginable.

Tucker blew out a breath that vibrated the speaker. "Looks like that's a good possibility. He has knowledge enough of the area to bury the bodies here. In a remote location that no one has uncovered for what looks like years. Now the rope is made locally. Add that he knew where to find Mia, and had knowledge of where to find you."

"Shit." He wobbled a little on his feet, and a strong hand on the small of his back steadied him.

Mia glanced up at him through long, black lashes. Concern clouding her eyes. "I got you," she whispered, taking his pole and placing it on the ground beside hers.

Chet cleared his throat. He kept his gaze locked on hers.

Words swam around in his head like the bobber still bouncing in the water, but none found their way out of his dry mouth.

"Lincoln wants to talk to Bobby," Tucker continued.

"I thought they spoke on the phone after the graves were discovered?"

"They did, but Lincoln had some questions that Eddy couldn't answer. Questions that told me Lincoln suspects Bobby might know more than he's let on."

Chet's stomach churned. "Bobby's on a cruise with his wife. He doesn't know a damn thing. And he can't be a suspect. He wasn't around when Mia was attacked, or the ropes were hung. Not to mention being out of the freaking state when Janie Simpson was murdered."

"Eddy lied."

The words exploded in Chet's brain like a bomb. "What?"

"Missy's been home for close to a week. Bobby went on a hunting trip. Alone. Eddy got scared when the graves were found on Bobby's land, so he said they were still on the cruise. Lincoln's pissed."

Chet scrubbed a hand over his face. "Anything else?" He couldn't take much more but needed to know if any more bad news awaited him.

"That's it for now. Lincoln's at the station going over the security feed from the store and running the receipts from the last couple weeks. Looking to see if anyone else purchased the rope that Eddy doesn't remember or didn't know about. I'm heading to the kennel. You okay? You or Mia need anything?"

He wasn't okay, but there wasn't a damn thing Tucker could do about it. "We're fine. Thanks for the update." Disconnecting, he kept the phone in his hand.

"I'd ask if everything is all right, but the look on your face is answer enough," Mia said.

"I need to sit."

Mia cupped a palm under his elbow and guided him down on the dock before settling beside him.

He rested the side of his head against the thick post that secured the dock. His feet dangled over the edge, the water almost reaching the soles of his boots. He needed to fill in Mia about what he'd learned but couldn't make out the sentences.

As if she understood he needed a minute to collect his thoughts, she slipped her hand in his and sat in the silence. Her sneakered-clad feet hanging beside his. "It sure is beautiful out here. I can't wait for summer. So far, I've seen a lot of snow and a lot of rain. I'm ready for the sun."

"Umm hmm."

"My hometown isn't far from here, but I never took the time to just sit outside and appreciate the beauty. I lived in town, worked in a factory, and spent my time focused on the future. Not really living in the moment. I need to do more of that."

"I've spent my time living in the past. Afraid to let go. Terrified of moving on." Pressure mounted in his chest. "I can't even get rid of this stupid phone." He hoisted the phone he still held in the air.

"It's important to keep pieces of the people we love with us. To take them into our future. That way, we never really move on. Moving on means we're over the loss and the pain and have no need for what we're moving on from to stay with us. Laurie and Riley should always be with you. Always be a part of your life, in any way that you need them. They made you the man you are today."

"They were amazing." His voice cracked, the pressure in his chest almost unbearable.

"I wish I could have met them," she said. "And anytime you want to introduce me to them, to share their stories or relive those wonderful moments, I'm ready to listen."

He bobbed his head, unable to speak. The voices of his beloved might have been a soothing balm for the past three years, but Mia brought something else into his life. Something he didn't even know he needed.

Mia brought hope. A feeling he'd given up on, and now that he had it again, he was terrified of losing it.

FOR THE SECOND time that day, Mia found herself bustling around Chet's kitchen. But this time, she didn't rummage through his pantry and refrigerator to put together a meal. Thanks to Wade, all she had to do was reheat the food he'd brought over earlier.

Chet hadn't spoken much since they'd returned inside. His mind was clearly occupied and keeping herself busy by plating their meals kept her from asking all the questions clamoring in her brain. "You want to eat at the table?"

Chet sat in the living room. Long shadows fell across the floor. Twilight had arrived, and Chet hadn't turned on any lights to fight against the darkening skies looming outside. He stood on a sigh and offered her a weak smile. "Sure. Thanks for this."

Carrying the full plates to the table, she placed one where Chet usually sat and the other across from him. Her stomach growled. She hadn't eaten much the last two days, and the scents of Wade's famous fried chicken and collard greens wafted to her, making her mouth water. "I didn't do much."

"You did plenty." He strolled across the kitchen and flipped open a cabinet. "Want some water? Beer?"

"I'd kill for a beer."

He hooked an eyebrow. "Really?"

"Yes, really."

"All right then. A beer for each of us." He closed the cabinet then grabbed two brown bottles from the fridge. He popped off the tops and offered her one then plopped down at his place at the head of the table.

She took a sip and the cold, bitter ale slid down her throat. Wine was her usual go to, but the beer tasted good after a long, awful day. "Thanks." Picking up the chicken leg, she took a bite, and the crispy skin filled her mouth. She closed her eyes, savoring the juicy meat and salty coating. "This is amazing."

"Wade knows his stuff. Smart, too. I'm convinced his chicken wouldn't taste as good if I could order it any day of the week."

She laughed and slid a bite of creamy potatoes in her mouth. Her mind went back to what Wade had said before leaving earlier. "Do you think he meant it?"

"Meant what? I couldn't hear him over all his damn flirting." A flash of red invaded his cheeks. He took a long pull of his beer.

"Jealous?" She preened with the possibility, no matter how crazy it seemed.

He grumbled something behind the beer.

"Seriously. Do you think Wade would talk about his business with me? I'll need all the help I can get if I want to open my own place one day." She peeled the blue and red label from the bottle. Unexpected nerves bustling in her stomach.

Chet lifted a shoulder. "Don't think he'd say it if he didn't mean it." He set his beer beside the blue place mat that matched the curtains hanging across the front window. "He's owned the Chill N' Grill for years. He'd have a lot to offer."

"Owning my own restaurant seems like such a distant dream now. Maybe I shouldn't waste his time." She sighed, her appetite suddenly gone.

"Don't give up on your dreams," Chet said. "Call Wade. See what he has to say. You never know how it might help."

She smiled, relieved to be discussing something other than the tragedies that had brought them together. "What about you? What are your dreams?"

Leaning back in his chair, he propped his feet up on the seat beside him. "Man, I haven't thought about that in a long time. My dreams all died with Laurie and Riley."

"I never met your wife, but something tells me she wouldn't want that."

The pinched expression on his face told her what she said was true. "I don't even know how to dream anymore— how to look toward the future and know better things lay ahead."

"Maybe it's time to try."

His heated gaze latched on her. "You might be right."

She shifted in her chair, unsure of what to say. Days before, she wouldn't have imagined her body would tremble with desire from just a simple look from Chet—that she'd long to hear him tell her that maybe he could have a future with her.

But was that what she really wanted? She'd been burned so recently that steam still flowed from the scars, and Chet had so much baggage that he hadn't even begun to process. Could she be the person to help him with that when her own wounds were so fresh?

"Are you not hungry?" Chet nodded toward her food, a glint of amusement shining from his eyes, as if he could read all the questions running on a hamster wheel in her mind.

She shrugged. "I have a lot on my mind."

"Such as?"

Not wanting to expose all her thoughts, she opted for the most pressing issue. "Just wondering about tonight. I'm still scared to be alone, but I don't want to intrude."

"You can stay again."

"Are you sure?"

He nodded then slipped a bite of potatoes between his lips.

The tingling sensation in her core shot her to her feet. If she was going to stay another night on his couch, she needed to get a grip. "I need more stuff. I'm going to run over to my place and grab a few things."

"Do you want me to come with you?"

Shaking her head, she hurried toward the door. "I'm fine. You're just a stone's throw away. Finish your meal. I'll be right back."

The fresh air outside slammed against her. She wished she could take a few minutes to let it cool her, but standing on her porch alone while the purple sky quickly turned black exposed her in a way she'd never realized before. Fishing out her keys, she let herself into her apartment. She flipped on every light in the place as she made her way to her bedroom. Her toiletries were already in Chet's bathroom. She just needed fresh pajamas and clothes to change into in the morning. Rifling through her drawers, she found clothes that were flattering but comfortable. An elbow-length tee that dipped down just a little at the neck and tight jeans.

A knock on her front door brought a smile to her lips. Leave it to Chet to insist to be by her side even when she'd sworn she'd be okay. She tossed her things in a tote bag she'd found in the closet, flipped the lights off in her room and hall as she stepped back into the living room.

The knock came again. More urgent this time. More demanding.

She rolled her eyes. Patience was not one of Chet's strong suits. "I was gone for two minutes," she teased, flinging open the door.

Aaron stood in the dim glow of the porch light. "Hi, honey. We need to talk."

14

A mixture of fear and anger swirled through Mia like a tornado. She tightened her grip on the door handle but straightened her spine. No way she'd let Aaron see the reaction he caused. "How did you find me?"

He huffed out a laugh, a placating look drawing his dark brows together. "What? Were you hiding?"

The smugness in his voice pushed aside her fear and made the anger burn brighter. "No, that was you, remember? After you stole everything from me."

He tilted his head to the side and pinched his full lips together. "I made a mistake, okay? Can I come in. We should talk."

She stood her ground, not letting his piercing blue eyes or the casual way he hooked his thumbs in the front pockets of his jeans fool her. He had an agenda. A big, whooping agenda if he showed up at her door and admitted to making a mistake. "We have nothing to discuss."

"Mia," he said, drawing out her name like he was speaking to a child. "Please. We were good together. We made plans—had a future waiting for us. Don't you want to see if we can get back what we had?"

She crossed her arms over her chest. "You didn't answer my question. How did you find me?"

He shrugged. "Your mom told me. When I explained my side of the story, she knew you'd want to speak with me."

Unshed tears burned behind her eyes, and she bit the insides of her cheeks to keep them from falling. Aaron would mistake her tears for joy over him when it was her mother's betrayal that cut her at her knees. "You should have called." She spoke with clenched teeth, using all her energy to keep her voice even.

"Showing up is a bigger gesture." He grinned, showing off straight white teeth.

"A bigger gesture than stealing, cheating, and running away?" She seethed and counted off each offense on the tips of her fingers.

Smacking his lips, Aaron sliced his hands through the air as if her argument was a silly whine he needed to squash. "Misunderstandings. Come on, babe."

"Don't call me that," she snapped. A thought dawned on her and made her stomach turn. "How long have you known I was here?"

"I talked to your mom yesterday."

So had she. Had her mom gone behind her back and told Aaron where she was even after she'd practically begged her mom to leave the situation alone. Confirmed, yet again, all the horrible things he'd done.

Well maybe not all of the horrible things. Some of the things she'd endured were too painful and humiliating to confess to anyone.

But even though her mama's willingness to give Aaron her personal information made her blood boil, a bigger question needed to be answered. Did Aaron know where she'd moved before her tires were slashed?

"When did you get into town?" She steeled her nerves for the blow his answer could deliver. Everyone had assumed the person responsible for vandalizing her vehicle was the killer. Maybe they'd all been wrong.

"What does it matter? I'm here now, and I want to make things right. I want to build that future we always wanted."

"It matters," she said.

He rocked back on his heels. "This morning. I needed to get up my nerve before talking to you."

She'd laugh at the absurdity of his answer as if it didn't terrify her. "You need to leave. Now."

"Stop being so dramatic." Aaron's chest puffed out as he drew in a large breath. The sound of crickets chirped in the distance, the pleasant cacophony of the springtime evening a direct contrast to the pissed-off snarl aimed her way.

His mask was slipping, along with his composure. She didn't want to be near him when they both fell away. "We're done here," she said, swinging the door closed.

Aaron shot out his hand and gripped the edge of the door, blocking it from closing. He pressed into her personal space, his breath hot against her face. "We're done when I say we're done. Let me in. Now."

She cringed at the pungent scent of liquor seeping from his pores. A beat of terror pulsed through her. "I said no." She slapped at his hand.

He took another step forward, forcing her back. Her heart pounded loudly in her ears. Aaron on a good day could be an ass, but he was completely unpredictable when drunk.

She shoved at his chest, and he latched onto her wrist.

Twisting it so she had to turn her body to the side. "Stop. You're hurting me."

"I wouldn't have to hurt you if you'd just listen to me."

The tiny hum of Chet's television leaked through the thin wall and snapped her into action. She wasn't alone. She didn't have to figure out how to get away from Aaron all by herself. "Chet!" She yelled his name as loud as she could. With the door open, and the barrier between their two apartments as thin as paper, he had to hear her.

Aaron's pale skin flushed red, his eyes wide and wild. He clamped a hand over her mouth, pushing her further into her apartment, then slammed the door closed.

She opened her mouth to yell again, but his sweaty palm swallowed her screams.

"What the hell is your problem? I came here to make things right." Each word was louder than the next. He increased the pressure on her mouth.

She winced then bit into his flesh. The tinny taste of blood flooded her mouth.

He dropped his hand. "You bitch." His swung back his uninjured hand then swiped it across her face, slapping her with his knuckles.

She stumbled away, shocked that he'd laid a hand on her. Her hands flew to her throbbing check. Panic increased her heart rate, and she darted her gaze around the room. Searching for the quickest escape. Tears stung her eyes, but this time, she couldn't do anything to stop them from falling.

He advanced, fury pinching his face. He raised his arm again.

The door burst open. Chet stormed inside and grabbed Aaron's forearm. He twisted the arm behind Aaron's back then slammed him against the wall. "Mia, call the police."

Worry softened his words, but he kept his body tight. His muscles rigid. "Are you okay?"

Fumbling for her phone, she nodded.

"Get off me," Aaron shouted. "Mia's not calling anyone. I'm her boyfriend, you idiot."

"Ex-boyfriend," she clarified.

Chet glanced at her with raised brows but didn't loosen his hold. "This the asshole?"

She nodded.

"Oh, she's definitely calling the police," Chet said, his voice more like a low growl. "Then she's charging you with assault."

The television droned on, the flickering of scenes lost on Chet. Rich women from some city screamed at each other for some petty reason or another—all just noise in the background. He'd never understand the draw of these types of shows, but he'd wanted Mia to be comfortable and had begrudgingly handed over the remote.

Unable to keep his attention off her, he glanced at her from the corner of his eye. A purple bruise had bloomed at the corner of her lip. An angry red mark from Aaron's hand surrounded her mouth. Hot anger rolled through him. He circled his fingers over one wrist, ringing his hand over and over until his tendons screamed.

"Stop watching me." Mia sat with her knees pressed to her chest, feet bare, and a blanket wrapped over her slim shoulders. She watched the chaos exploding on the screen as she scolded him.

"Well I can't watch whatever this crap is." He flicked his

wrist toward the television mounted above the fireplace. "How is it fun to watch people fight?"

Grinning, she shrugged. "It's mind-numbing. I can just turn off my brain and not think and get lost in someone else's drama for a little bit."

"Hmm," he said, shifting his focus to the show. "Never thought about it like that. Laurie used to watch this show."

"It's like cat nip." Mia picked up her wine glass and took a sip.

He didn't keep wine at his place, never drank the stuff, but she'd grabbed a bottle from her place after the police had hauled off Aaron and taken her statement. She'd trembled the entire time, and he was proud as hell that she'd stood her ground. He'd witnessed enough domestic abuse cases to know how difficult it was for some women to stand up to their abusers. To press charges and do everything they could to stop the person hurting them.

Now, Aaron could sit in a jail cell until everything was sorted. His job was to be here for Mia. Even if that meant watching shitty TV. "Can I get you anything?"

A commercial came on, and she shifted so her back was pressed against the arm of the couch. "I'm good."

"Feeling okay?"

She lifted her fingertips to her cracked lip and winced. "Fine."

"You're swelling a little. You need ice." He jumped to his feet and found a plastic bag stuffed in a drawer. He filled it with ice, wrapped a towel around the bag, then brought it to her. "Here ya go."

"Thanks," she said, gently placing the cloth on her mouth. She tensed then extended one leg, tucking her foot under her knee.

He lowered back down on the couch, sitting a little

closer to Mia than he had been. He was drawn to her like a magnet, needing to do whatever he could to make her feel better. "Has he ever hit you before?"

"No." She shifted the cream-colored blanket to cover her lap.

Her answer surprised him. If he'd have just gone with her to pack, Aaron wouldn't have hit her tonight either. But the energy between them had sizzled so hot, he'd been relieved when she'd left him alone for a few minutes. He found himself blurting out so many unexpected things around her, like he couldn't control the filter between his brain and his mouth. "I'm sorry."

"You have nothing to apologize for. You showed up again, my knight in shining armor. I still can't believe he found me. That he thought I'd just let him talk his way out of everything he did and just pick up where we left off." She swapped her ice for the wine and took another sip.

"Was he always a dick?" He shouldn't pry but couldn't help himself. How did a relationship unravel? How could someone hide their true colors for so long?

Sighing, she shook her head. "Aaron is a textbook narcissist. Obviously, that's something I didn't realize until I was already sucked into his toxic vortex. When we first met, he swept me off my feet. Literally. It was raining and I slipped on a wet patch of cement. He came out of nowhere and caught me. From that moment on, he made it his mission to take care of me."

Chet ran his tongue over his teeth, his insides twisting. Her description of her previous relationship didn't sound like something she regretted, which made the glaring marks he put on her face even uglier. "Sounds like a peach."

She kicked out her foot, and he captured it in his hand.

She didn't pull away or object to his touch, so he kept his hand wrapped around her cool skin.

Swallowing hard, she continued. "Over time, I realized he wasn't trying to take care of me but control me. When I'd demand to do things my way, he'd insist I couldn't do it right. When I argued with him, he'd treat me like a child. Every move he made was a deliberate attack on my confidence. He crippled me emotionally, abused me verbally, and when I finally had enough, he found someone else—while we were dating—and took off with all my money and possessions."

Fury clenched Chet's jaw. No matter how much of an ass he'd been to Mia since she started working at the retreat, she always showed up with a smile. Always helped him anyway she could. She was kind and sweet and caring. She didn't deserve to be treated poorly. "I'm glad you didn't tell me this before. I would have had to put my fist in the guy's face."

She smiled and sunk deeper against the side of the couch.

Without thinking, he moved his fingers against the arch of her foot, gently kneading. "Why didn't you have him arrested for theft?"

"Both our names were on the account. His idea," she said, an irritated smirk on her lips. "Besides, I didn't know where he went, and I had no desire to find him. I want him out of my life. He's slippery. Manipulative and sneaky. I don't need that around."

"Do you think he slashed your tires?"

She shrugged. "I honestly don't know. He acted like he didn't know what I was talking about when I brought it up to Beau, but Aaron is a world-class liar."

He moved one hand up to Mia's ankle, digging into her

toned muscles. As he rubbed away her tension, his own melted away. "Is he capable?"

"Before today, I don't know if I would have said yes. But after what he just did...how he acted. I just feel so stupid for getting myself into this situation. For letting him dupe me then not getting away from him sooner. I can't believe I let things get so bad." She sniffed back the tears filling her eyes.

"Hey. Don't cry." He hooked his arm under her knees and brought her closer. Tears were his kryptonite, and watching Mia beat herself up over something that wasn't her fault was torture. He wrapped his arm around the small of her back and the smell of her coconut shampoo tickled his senses.

She buried her head in his chest. "I'm sorry. This is the last thing you need to be worried about."

"You're the only thing I'm worried about right now. You have every right to be upset. You trusted this man. Loved him."

She pulled back, tilting her chin to look up at him, and sadness weighed down her features. "I don't even know what love is."

He hitched up the corner of his mouth. "Yes, you do."

"What makes you say that?"

"Because you show it to people every day. It's in your food. How you treat people. Hell, even with me. I've been such a jerk, but you still took care of me. That's love."

"But I've never been *in* love. Not like what you had with Laurie. Where you find someone you give your whole heart. That you cherish more than yourself. You're lucky." Her eyes rounded. "I'm so sorry. That didn't come out right."

He smiled. "I was lucky. I loved Laurie more than life itself. Still do. I wouldn't trade that for anything. Even with all the pain. Even if I don't know who I am without her."

He'd floundered like a lost ship, being tossed around from wave to wave, in an endless sea. No anchor. No destination. No idea what life meant without the two people he loved the most.

"I know exactly who you are." Her gaze landed on his mouth.

The soft hush of her words heated his core. He stopped the motions of his hands, the moment suddenly becoming intimate. Special. As if what she was about to say could change everything between them. "And who is that?" He inched closer to her. Her warm breath caressed his cheeks. The need to kiss her, to take her mouth in his, almost overpowered him. He licked his lips but didn't push any further. He didn't want to take advantage, and hell, he was scared. He hadn't kissed a woman in so long, he feared he'd forgotten how.

Mia cupped her palm against his rough beard. "You're the man who's been through the unthinkable but still shows up. Still gives his all. Who's made me feel safe and protected and like everything's going to be okay...no matter how much things may seem otherwise. You're Chet. I'm lucky that life has put you in my path. And I'm grateful."

Leaning forward, she gently pressed her lips to his then pulled away, a smile on her face. "Now. Let's forget about all the bad stuff for just a little while and keep watching this really awful show."

A booming laugh burst from his mouth, a sound so foreign and so wonderful. His heart swelled and the taste of her soft lips was seared in his brain. With his arm around her shoulders, he nestled her to his side and pretended like the worst thing happening in his life was having to watch the ridiculous women throwing drinks at each other on the TV.

15

The smell of sizzling bacon lifted Mia's eyelids. A yawn ripped through her mouth, and she stretched her arms high over her head. Her hand smacked against the end table beside Chet's couch and jostled the lamp.

Hurrying to a sitting position to steady the lamp before it fell, she peered over the back of the couch to find Chet busy in the kitchen. Coffee dripped into a half-filled pot, its scent combined with the bacon and made her mouth water.

Chet turned with a sheepish grin. "Morning."

She ran her hands through her hair, aware of her rumpled appearance. Oh God, her breath had to be horrible.

He chuckled. "You look beautiful."

Heat swept into her cheeks. He'd told her not too long ago he could read her. Now she wondered if he could actually see into her mind. As much as the idea was unnerving, the compliment calmed her silly nerves.

"I'm not used to such flattery so early in the morning." She puckered her brow. "Or ever for that matter."

Chet clicked his tongue. "That's a shame."

She stood and joined him in the kitchen. A bowl of cracked eggs sat on the counter beside a pan of what looked like cake batter. Cinnamon swirls topped the creamy batter —coffee cake. "Looks like you're preparing a feast."

He reached above his head for cooking spray and a tiny patch of skin appeared between his shirt and the waistband of his sweatpants.

Her mouth watered for a completely different reason.

"Felt like cooking." He threw a smile over his shoulder. "Didn't know what you'd be in the mood for."

His consideration warmed her to her toes. A man had never cooked her breakfast before. Let alone pulled out all the contents of his fridge to make sure he made something she'd like. "Need any help?"

"Nope. Grab some coffee. Relax." He nudged a mug forward that he'd placed on the counter by the pot.

She filled her mug then sat at the table, watching him. Studying the broad set of his shoulders and tapered waist. His pants hung low on his hips, and she itched to run her fingers over the abs she'd seen the day before.

Oh sheesh, his stitches. Between Aaron showing up and then kissing Chet last night—God she kissed him—she'd forgotten he was the injured one. That a murderer had sliced him with a knife. "How's your side?"

"Fine," he said, flipping the bacon. "How's your lip?"

She lifted her fingertips to the corner of her mouth. A sharp pain throbbed from her touch. "Okay, as long as nothing's touching it."

He glanced her way with raised brows.

She wrinkled her nose, embarrassment flushing her face. "You know what I mean."

Turning back to the stove, he chuckled.

The sound of a car door slamming turned her head to the window. Tucker stalked toward the apartment, an unfamiliar frown on his face and a dog at his heels. Confusion brought her to her feet, opening the door wide. "Is that my car?"

"Morning." Tucker hurried up the porch stairs and offered her shoulder a quick squeeze before stepping over the threshold. "Yep. Cruz released it last night. He's heading this way to take me back to the station."

The gray and black mutt ran past her while she stared, slack-jawed and bewildered, at her car. Washed and shiny with four new tires in the drive. "I...I don't understand," she said, shutting the door and facing the kitchen. "How did my car get new tires?"

Chet kept cooking while Tucker helped himself to a piece of bacon then filled a mug. The dog sat next to Chet, tail thumping against the floor.

"Umm, excuse me?" She fisted her hands on her hips.

Tucker took a bite of bacon and shrugged. "I just followed orders."

"Whose orders?"

He flipped the bacon over his shoulder at Chet. "He's to thank for the tires. I brought you Wrigley."

She rubbed circles over her temple as she tried to keep up with the conversation. She hadn't even had a drop of coffee yet. "Wait. One thing at a time. Chet, did you tell Tucker to put tires on my car?"

Finally, he faced her. His shoulders drooped, and he scrunched his face like a child who was afraid of being reprimanded after spilling the truth. "Yes."

"Why did you do that?"

He lifted his palms. "You need good tires. I'm sorry if I overstepped. I should have asked."

Touched, she crossed the room and wrapped her arms around his waist, hugging him close. Gratitude wedged in her throat. Tears threatened to fill her eyes, but she sniffed them back.

Chet lowered to speak in her ear. "I wasn't trying to control you."

His words made her smile. He remembered their conversation from last night and was concerned that his actions would be perceived the same as Aaron's manipulative behavior. But this was nothing like Aaron. Putting tires on her car didn't benefit Chet at all. Except he didn't need to drive her around anymore.

"I was just trying to help," he whispered.

"Thank you." She lifted onto her toes and kissed his bearded cheek.

Tucker cleared his throat, drawing both of their attention.

She aimed her sweetest smile at him. "Okay. Now tell me about Wrigley."

At the sound of his name, the medium-sized dog jumped to all fours and barked once.

"Wrigley's new," Tucker said, not bothering to hide his amused smirk and questioning eyes. "He was being fostered by a buddy of mine who made sure to get all of his certifications for being a therapy dog. I planned to use him at the retreat, but I thought you might like to have him."

"Me?" She loved spending time with the dogs at the kennel, but she'd never owned an animal of her own. She didn't even know if she was allowed to keep a pet in her apartment.

Tucker carried his steaming mug to the table and sat. "Otto made you feel safe, but I need him with me. The other dogs have strict schedules I like to keep as much as possible.

But Wrigley here, he needs a home. Some special attention. And he's trained. He can protect you."

"I can protect her," Chet growled.

She smoothed his chest with her palm then lowered to her haunches. "Come here, boy."

Wrigley bounded to her. His butt wiggled, and he licked her face.

She giggled. "Sit."

He obeyed.

She ran her hand over his head and down his side. "What kind of dog is he?"

"German Short-Haired Pointer. He's a sweet boy. A little over a year. What do you think?"

Wrigley lurched forward, pushing her to the ground, then sat in her lap.

"Does Bobby allow pets?" She asked Chet.

He groaned. "Probably."

She aimed narrowed eyes his way. "What's with the groan?"

"Dogs shed and bark and shit in the yard."

"You like Otto," she countered. "And besides, I'm the one who'll deal with the mess. He'd be my dog, at my place. Not yours."

Something flashed on his face, as if her words somehow hurt him, then he scooped up the baking pan and shoved it in the oven.

Gravel crunched outside followed by the slamming of a car door.

"Sounds like Cruz is here to pick me up," Tucker said. "Elizabeth is on her way to the police station. I told her I'd meet her."

Chet tensed. "Want me there?"

"Nah, let's give her some time to get settled. She'll let you know when she wants to talk to you. To both of you."

A knock rattled the door before Cruz let himself in. "Morning guys. How's it going?"

Wrigley barked, but stayed seated by Mia.

Chet grunted.

Mia stood, smiling. "Okay. How's Aaron?" She didn't care how her ex was faring as much as wondered what would happen to him now that she'd pressed charges for assault.

"He's out on bail with instructions to leave you alone. If he contacts you or tries to see you, call me."

She nodded. "Thanks."

"Ready, Tucker?" Cruz asked.

Tucker stood, grabbing his mug and taking a big gulp. "Yep. Mia, I'll leave dishes and food on the porch for Wrigley. Chet, I'll be in touch."

Wrigley whined and ran to the window overlooking the porch, watching the men leave.

She waved and leaned against the counter, watching Chet for a few moments. He mixed and flipped and stirred, wordlessly assembling their meal with ease. "Are you upset about the dog? I can tell Tucker no."

"I hate that you need a dog to protect you." The oven dinged, and he slid out a tray of rolls.

The catch in his voice surprised her. "Are you sure that's all it is?"

Sighing, he set down his spatula and shoved a hand through his messy hair. "I never let Riley have a dog. I spouted off those same damn reasons. This isn't the same. This is your dog, your life, your place. I don't have a say. But in that moment, I heard myself telling her no. Saw the disappointment in her eyes. I should have let her have a puppy."

"Oh, Chet." She embraced him, a position that was starting to feel more natural than breathing.

He dropped his chin to the top of her head. "You should keep Wrigley. And we should eat."

"You think Bobby will be okay with it?" Hope lifted her voice as the idea of owning the adorable pooch grew on her.

"We'll head to town and ask Missy. Besides, I have some questions for her."

She inhaled, breathing in the scents of the freshly cooked breakfast and Chet's soap. They'd have one more moment of peace, of normalcy, before tackling the pile of crap awaiting them.

CHET WIPED his hands on the thighs of his jeans before climbing out of his truck. His palm still tingled where Mia's hand had rested against his. He held her hand the whole way into town, and he needed to shake the feelings of excitement and a giddiness he hadn't experienced since he was a teenager before they spoke with Missy Truly. His head wouldn't be on straight if he kept wondering what the rest of Mia's body felt like.

Wispy clouds dotted the blue sky. The sun peeking between the white spots. April needed to make up its damn mind. Rain or sun. Today he'd choose to be grateful for the lack of moisture falling from the sky.

Mia met him at the front of the truck. Wrigley followed behind her. "Does Missy know we're here?"

He nodded. "I didn't want to just show up out of the blue. I didn't tell her about the dog though. Figured it'd be harder to say no with the mutt in her face. She's always had a soft spot for animals. Hates that Bobby hunts."

The mention of one of Bobby's favorite pastimes brought back the real reason he'd wanted to talk with Missy. According to Tucker, Eddy had confessed his lie of Bobby's whereabouts to protect his uncle—who was hunting alone at the time in question. With no alibi and spotty reception which made it impossible for Lincoln or Cruz to get ahold of him. But Missy might have some answers that could help find Bobby, as well as clues regarding any suspicions around him. Because there was no way in hell Bobby was the man they were looking for.

The maple door with an etched glass window in the center swung open, and Missy clapped her hands under her chin. At close to seventy, she still stood tall and proud. Gray hair brushed the tops of her broad shoulders. She wiped her hands on a white apron tied around her waist that hid the the top half of her blue and yellow floral dress. "Mornin' you two. Just pulled out some muffins to share over coffee."

Chet strode toward Missy and pulled her into a hug. "You should't have," he said, pressing a quick kiss to her plump cheek.

"Nonsense." She slapped his shoulder then aimed a sweet smile at Mia. "Besides, I still need to get to know this young lady. And ain't nothing better than chatting over fresh baked goods."

"I couldn't agree more, ma'am." Mia extended a hand. "We've met once before, but it's nice to see you again."

Missy grabbed her hand, resting her free palm over Mia's knuckles. "No ma'am's around her, dear. Call me Missy. Who is this big guy?"

"He's one of the reasons we're here," Chet said, cringing inwardly about the upcoming conversation. Based on Missy's demeanor, either no one had spoken with her about what'd been going on, or she didn't quite understand how bad this situation was.

Missy rooted her fists on her hips. "One of the reasons?"

Not wanting to get into the details standing in the tiny postage stamp of a yard, surrounded by neighbors, he dipped his chin toward the door. "Let's head inside."

Missy gave an exaggerated sigh and led the way. "Muffins are getting cold anyway."

Chet waited for Mia and Wrigley to step inside before following, closing the door behind them. Just like Missy's floral frock and Bobby's denim overalls, nothing had changed about the Truly's home in years. Glass figurines cluttered the built-in bookcases in the living room, the same furniture his own grandparents had owned all faced an old tube television, and photos of Missy and Bobby's daughter who'd died tragically in her twenties hung on the walls.

He never doubted Bobby and Missy's own loss was one of the things that had softened Chet's heart to the older couple—and opened their arms to him. Understanding someone else's pain brought about a brotherhood that no one wants to be a part of.

Mia glanced over her shoulder as she followed Missy down the narrow hallway that led to the kitchen. Wrigley stayed glued to her side. Her raised brow asked an unspoken question.

Chet nodded, understanding she wanted to make sure he was all right. The knots in his gut might say otherwise, but he hoped those knots would slip away after this conversation.

Missy scooted around the kitchen, shuttling coffee cups, plates, and food to the square table that sat in the middle of the room. "Go on now. Take a seat."

Knowing she'd refuse any offered help, he did as directed.

Mia settled in the chair beside him. "It smells amazing in here."

Missy beamed. "Thank you, dear. Old family recipe." She placed a napkin on each plate, filled their mugs, then finally took a seat, her gaze pinned on the dog. "Spill it."

"A friend dropped this dog off for me earlier," Mia explained. "I wasn't sure if I was allowed to have a dog in my apartment, and Chet suggested we stop by and ask."

Missy arched her penciled in brows sky-high. "Oh did he?"

Chet squirmed in his chair.

"If it's a problem, I'll give the dog back. It's no big deal." Mia rambled, her words spilling out.

Missy patted her hand. "It's not that dear. Bobby and I don't mind if you own an animal as long as you take care of the sweet thing and make sure he doesn't destroy anything. What I don't understand is why Chet wouldn't just pick up the phone."

Chet fought a grin. Missy wasn't one to beat around the bush. A trait he both appreciated and despised. "Where's Bobby?"

Missy stiffened her spine. "Hunting."

"Since when?"

"Three nights ago. He took off as soon as we got home. He hated being trapped on that boat and needed to stretch his legs, he said." She nibbled the top of her muffin then washed it down with a sip of coffee. "I mean, there was plenty of space to walk on the ship. But you know Bobby. Have you ever been on a cruise, dear?" She aimed the question at Mia.

Mia smiled. "No, ma'am."

"Missy, we need to talk to Bobby. It's important," Chet said, cutting to the heart of the matter. He didn't like the way she tried to change the subject. As if she were hiding something.

She waved away his worry. "He'll come 'round when he's ready."

"Have you spoken with the police? Eddy?" He took a bite of his muffin. Cinnamon and sugar melted in his mouth, and the tart taste of warm blueberries exploded on his tongue.

Missy sighed. "Yes, and yes. I like Cruz, but that brother of his doesn't understand the way things work here. I can't just call Bobby and tell him to come home."

"Does Bobby know what was found on his property?" Mia asked. "I'm sure he'd want to be as cooperative as possible if he understood what was at stake."

Missy fiddled with the front of her apron, refusing to make eye contact with either one of them. "I don't know if Bobby knows or not."

The deliberate way in which she weighed her words set Chet on edge. "What do you mean?"

Tears filled Missy's eyes. "I don't know where he is. I haven't seen him in about two weeks."

Mia's jaw dropped. "What about the cruise?"

Missy shrugged, finally lifting her gaze to meet his. "He didn't want to go, and I refused to stay. Refused to miss out on my dream. I came home to a note he was hunting and would be back soon."

The muffin turned to lead in Chet's stomach. Bobby hadn't just been gone for a couple nights, he'd been gone for weeks. With no witnesses, no communication, and no alibi.

16

After forcing down half of her muffin and enduring a few more tense questions for Missy Truly, a call from Cruz had Mia and Chet sitting in the break room at the police station. Empathy made leaving Missy with her worries and questions difficult, but Mia had nothing to offer the older woman to ease the burden on her shoulders. At least Mrs. Truly had been pleased to watch Wrigley while they made their unexpected pit stop at the station. Hopefully the dog would give her a small amount of comfort for an hour or two.

Now, she sat beside Chet on a hard folding chair that had been brought in to accommodate the cluster of people working the case. The station didn't boast a conference room, and the two offices were way too small to fit everyone. Instead, the crew gathered chairs in a circle on the white linoleum floor. The buzz of the overhead lighting competed with the hum of the old refrigerator, the smell of microwave popcorn heavy in the air.

"Thanks for stopping by so quickly," Cruz said. He'd shoved the small table against the wall, his chair tucked up beside it. File folders were stacked one on top of another. "I'd like you both to meet Elizabeth Gilmore, former FBI profiler."

The woman who stood in the corner with straight, blonde hair that barely skimmed the top of her shoulders offered a stiff smile. "Good afternoon. I asked Cruz to gather everyone here so I can get a better understanding of what we're working with. I've poured over the case files, current and past ones, and now want to learn from you all."

Chet shifted in his seat.

Nervous energy practically vibrated his skin. Mia rested a steady palm on his forearm, wanting to comfort him despite her own nerves dancing in her belly.

Tucker sat at Elizabeth's side. He leaned back in his chair with an ankle hooked over his knee. Otto laid on the floor by his chair. "We appreciate you coming, Elizabeth. And to everyone else, I know I'm no longer an officer of the law, but I appreciate you letting me sit in today. I want to help in any way I can, even if it's by chauffeuring Lizzie around town."

A light blush stained Elizabeth's pale cheeks. She pivoted, showing more of her back to Tucker. "So far, the only clear-cut connection between our known victims is that both Janie Simpson and Laurie Black attended the same university, and both had taken a class taught by Professor Leonard Lipton."

Chet's entire body tensed at the name. "Has anyone talked to him?"

Lincoln nodded. "I did."

"And?"

Lincoln met Chet's stare head on, his jaw set tight under his scruffy jaw. "No alibi for the night Janie Simpson died."

Mia scooted to the edge of her seat. "What about when

my tires were slashed, or the ropes were tied in the tree in our yard?"

Lincoln shook his head. "Nothing concrete."

Deflated, Mia slouched against her chair as if the air had been stolen from her lungs. Having or not having an alibi didn't make Professor Lipton a serial killer, but it didn't look good. A mixture of emotion swelled like a giant wave inside her. She had sat in this man's class twice a week for three months. Could she really have read him so poorly?

Shoving a hand through his hair, Chet shot to his feet. "Damn it, arrest him. Haul his ass here. What more do you need? A signed confession? If you let me talk to the sonofabitch, I'll get him to confess. I promise you that."

"You know you can't talk to him," Cruz said, cradling a paper cup in his hands. "And you know that yes, we need more than just not being able to verify his whereabouts to charge him with murder."

Chet lifted his hands and muttered under his breath.

"Gentlemen, please," Elizabeth said. "I understand there are a lot of moving parts to any investigation, but for this moment, I would like to focus on motive. On patterns. On asking questions about the victims so I can get inside this man's head." She crossed through the makeshift circle of chairs. Her heels clicked across the floor. She smoothed her slender hands over the black jacket she'd paired over a classic white shirt then swiped the top file from the stack on the table. "Mr. Black. I'd like to ask you some questions about your wife's case."

Staying on his feet, Chet crossed his arms over his chest. "Fine."

"I understand that Laurie left the house the evening she was murdered in order to turn in a paper to Professor Lipton. A paper that was due the day before, but the professor had granted an extension because of extenuating circumstances."

"Correct."

"And you were out of town that night?"

Chet nodded.

A ball of anxiety sat in Mia's gut. Chet had confided the basics of what had happened to his family, but she didn't know the details. Heck, she didn't really want to know the details. Especially not like this, with him answering questions thrown at him by a stranger in a group of people in a cold room. But she didn't have a choice except to sit and listen and hope that whatever came from this conversation brought a new perspective.

"Did Professor Lipton know you were out of town?" Elizabeth kept her face a smooth mask as she peppered Chet with painful questions.

"I don't know."

She scanned the file then used her pointer finger to mark her place in some unseen spot. "According to this, your wife left the house around 5:45 pm in the evening, after speaking with you on the phone, taking your daughter with her. She turned in her paper, which is supported by Professor Lipton. At that point, no one else spoke with your wife or daughter or saw them, until you returned home unexpectedly and found your wife and daughter bound in your bedroom."

Bile slid up Mia's esophagus. She wanted to run from the room, to cover her ears, to turn away and not hear the horrible truth that was Chet's nightmare.

Nodding, Chet worked his tightened jaw back and forth.

"Why would someone bring them back to the house? Why would Professor Lipton kidnap them at the college then drive them home? Unless he knew your whereabouts, he'd be risking a lot."

"Why would anyone?" Chet shot back, voice as hard as the metal folding chair Mia sat on.

Elizabeth hooked an eyebrow. "That's the question of the hour. Or at least one of them." She scooped up another file and flipped it open. "The other would be why did this man kill your wife and daughter the same night he took them? Hours after. The assumption appears to be that you came home, startled him, he attacked you and fled after bounding you, and left you all in the home to burn."

Mia squeezed her eyes shut against the ghostly image.

"That's correct," Cruz said, filling in the answer after several beats of silence.

"But why not make sure to kill you, too? Why not take your wife and daughter somewhere he has more knowledge of, more certainty and privacy so he can treat them the same as every other victim that has been discovered?" Elizabeth kept her words measured, quiet, and calm. As if she were trying to answer them herself as she asked them.

Chet stayed silent and the air in the room crackled with emotional energy.

"We don't know," Tucker said, voicing what had to be in everyone else's mind. "What's your initial thought? I know you have one."

The mask of professionalism finally slipped from Elizabeth's face and sadness pooled in her hazel eyes. "What happened with Laurie and Riley was more personal. It wasn't just a random woman and child. It wasn't planned. He'd thought about taking them—at least Laurie—before. He knew them. And he knows you, Chet. Because if he didn't, you would be dead."

~

COLD CONDENSATION COATED Chet's palms, but the heat of
anger still pulsed inside him with every rapid beat of his
heart. The Chill N' Grill was mostly empty in the late afternoon. A few stragglers lingered at tables, stretching out their
lunch hours before returning to whatever job made them
wear a suit and tie. The low thrum of music was just a
jumble of words and noises in Chet's ears.

Mia sat on a backless stool to his left side, Cruz on the
other, but the only thing in his mind was the litany of opinions Elizabeth Gilmore had dropped on him like a grenade.
If what she said was right, then not only was the killer from
Pine Valley, but it was someone he knew. Which not only
ruled out Professor Lipton, but made Chet consider
everyone in town a suspect. Something that left him unsettled at least, pissed off and fearful at most.

But as much as he didn't want to admit it, what Elizabeth
said made sense. Especially considering the photo found of
Laurie and Riley and the personal attacks on him and Mia
since the graves were uncovered. As if by simply being
present when the victims had been found had reopened
some personal vendetta Chet had known nothing about.

"Well, Tucker's profiler definitely didn't pull any punch-
es," Cruz said, lifting a finger to signal to Wade. "How ya
feeling, man?"

Chet lifted his glass to his lips and drained his beer.
"Like I need another drink."

Wade grabbed his glass and placed it under the tap,
pulling the wooden lever to fill the cup with the amber
liquid. "You guys need anything else?"

"Just the check." Cruz slid his empty plate forward. Only
a few French fries left behind.

Mia pushed aside a salad she'd barely touched. "I'm good, Wade. Thanks."

Chet waited for his now-full glass and took another swig. Previous experience had shown him no amount of alcohol would dim his pain, but damnit, he needed something to take off the edge.

Wade placed a slip of paper in front of Cruz. "I'll be in the back. Holler if ya'll need me."

Chet stared into his glass. Speaking with Elizabeth had brought to life even more haunting memories. Memories he wished had burned along with his house three years ago.

Mia propped her elbows on the bar. "She seemed so certain of everything she said. How can she read some statements, talk to strangers, then come up with such concrete theories about what's going on in some madman's brain?"

Cruz shrugged and plucked his wallet from the back pocket of his jeans. "She was one of the top profilers in the country. I don't understand the complexities of everything that goes into what she does, but the students she's teaching right now don't realize how lucky they are to have her. And when you pick apart what she has to say, it's hard to argue with her conclusion."

"If we follow her train of thought, it would mean that whoever took Laurie and Riley knew that Chet was out of town that night. Was there anyone you or Laurie told?" Mia asked.

Pain beat against the middle of his forehead. He'd been over all of this so many times before. Desperation made him want to believe talking things through one more time would lead to answers, but chances of that happening were as low as the beer level at the bottom of his glass. "It wasn't a secret I was gone."

"Was it just for a night?" Mia asked.

He scrubbed a palm over his face. "A few. My mom had died a month before. I had to close up her house and get it ready for sale. The guys I worked with knew where I was. Laurie's friends. Hell, it's Pine Valley. Shit gets around fast. Even mundane info. Half the town probably knew where I was, and when I was supposed to get home."

"Is there anyone who asked a lot of questions about when you'd be back?" Mia asked. "Or talked to your wife about it? Anyone who'd bothered her, or even stood out as being a little too friendly?"

He thought back on the conversations he'd had with Laurie while he'd been out of town. Tried to remember her mentioning anything, or anyone, bothering her. Only one name came to mind. "Professor Lipton." He drained his beer then signaled a waitress for his bill.

"I had Wade put yours and Mia's stuff on my bill," Cruz said, standing. "I hate dragging this all back up. I really do. But Professor Lipton doesn't fit the profile Elizabeth has started building."

"Doesn't make him innocent." Chet didn't want to appear unappreciative of the favor Tucker had called in. Hell, he understood all too well how much it cost Tucker to call his old friend's widow. But if Professor Lipton—a man who had repeatedly hit on his wife, knowing she was married—wasn't guilty, it meant someone he knew was. The thought soured the beer in his gut. "I gotta get out of here."

Without waiting for Mia or Cruz, he stalked across the old wooden planks. He kept his head down, pushing through the door and gulping in fresh air to keep from throwing up. Gravel crunched under his boots as he crossed the lot to his truck. He just needed a few minutes away from everyone and everything to get his bearings before driving Mia home.

Yanking open the driver's side door, his gaze caught on something small and fluffy sitting in the middle of the bench seat. A red cowboy hat sat on the top of its head, and it had only one little beady black eye.

Riley's teddy bear.

The world tilted, his head spinning, and the sour beer churned in his stomach before shooting up into the back of his throat. He ran to the edge of the lot, purging the contents of his stomach.

If only he could expel everything else eating him up inside as easily.

17

Chet's head spun. The last few days, his life had been caught in a disgusting pattern—horrifying discovery followed by no evidence to shine a light on the person responsible. No witnesses or clues or as much as a freaking shadow to point him in the right direction.

Because right now, the only direction he wanted to go was straight home. Where he could draw the shades and hide away from the world. Sit in the solitude he'd craved for so long yet had alluded him since the day Mia slid down a hill and uncovered a shallow grave.

Instead, he sat inside the Chill N' Grill while people bustled around him. Taking statements and discussing video footage that didn't show a thing. Pressure squeezed his chest and the pain in his heart had him hunching over the table. His scars burned, and he grasped his wrists, pressing his fingers into the raised flesh in a futile attempt to make it stop. To make the pain, the memories, the assault on his damn life stop.

He squeezed his eyes shut against the agony ripping into his soul, but the faces of everyone he'd loved and lost flashed across his mind, forcing his eyes open again. Mia and Zoe sat at the table with him, but for the first time in the last couple of days, Mia's presence did nothing but suffocate him and remind him that he had no right doing whatever the hell it was they were doing. If history had taught him anything, it was that the people he cared about most where the ones who met the most violent ends.

And he could do nothing to protect them.

Lincoln marched between empty tables, shoving aside chairs in his way, coming to a halt in front of Chet. "I'm so sorry, man."

The weight of despair sat heavily on his shoulders, stealing his ability to move. To speak. To even think. So he sat, staring at the mounted buck head above the stone fireplace.

"Did you find anything at all?" Mia asked.

Lincoln shook his head.

"I've got to get out of here." Chet staggered to his feet. He gripped the edge of the table as he swayed.

Mia shot up and rounded the corner. She cupped his elbow in her palm. "Here. Let me help."

Her touch sent waves of guilt and shame down his arm, and he jerked away. "I'm fine."

She flinched and dropped her gaze to the floor but didn't say a word.

Good. He didn't need her spewing out words of comfort. Meaningless sentiments wouldn't do him any good right now. Not when his heart was shattering. Not when his arms ached to hold Riley again, but all he had left was the scuzzy teddy bear that his daughter used to drag around every-where. But even the bear was encased in an evidence bag, beyond his reach.

Zoe cleared her throat. "Mia, do you want to come hang

with me and Brooke for a little bit? We're thinking about adding a spin class for the guests at the retreat, and if I like it, I might even make room for some bikes at the studio. We plan to attend a class this afternoon. I'd love to get another opinion."

Relief sagged Chet's shoulders. He didn't have the energy to worry about Mia right now. Hell, he barely had the energy it'd take to walk out of here and get his ass home. Once he was there, all he wanted was to be left alone. And not even the shock of hurt in Mia's eyes could change his mind.

"Sure," Mia said, forcing a tight smile. "I'll need to grab some clothes. But a workout sounds like the perfect way to clear my mind."

"Call me if you find anything," Chet said. Not wanting to face any more questions or pity or disappointment, he marched past the cluster of people all wanting to help, none of whom could do anything. Because at the end of the day, nothing would bring back his family. Nothing would put his daughter back in his arms. And nothing would knit the broken pieces of his heart back together. He pushed out the door and narrowed his gaze at his truck.

Dread fisted his throat. Another part of him violated. Another treasured item broken into and tarnished. A burst of determination straightened his spine. He didn't want to sit in that truck and feel the presence of the asshole who tormented him. He wanted to find that asshole and make him pay.

Needing to make his head right and calm down, he opted to turn toward the mountain road that ran in front of the restaurant and straight into town. He'd walk, giving himself a few moments alone and the peace of the cool spring day to let his nerves settle. He'd focus on the beams of sun streaming through the blossoming trees, warming his skin, and the slopes of the mountain peaks.

Then he'd switch gears and stop pissing around with ridiculous thoughts of a future with Mia or hope that someday his life would get better. None of that mattered right now. All that mattered was justice for his family, and one way or another, he'd get it.

He might not have all the answers, but the first place he needed to go was Truly's Trading Post to speak with Eddy. Eddy had already lied once about Bobby's whereabouts. Chances were high he'd do it again. And right now, Chet was tired of the bullshit. He'd get the answers he needed out of Eddy if he had to squeeze them out of his skinny neck. Because as much as it killed him to admit it, right now, Bobby was looking more suspicious by the second.

AFTER A QUICK CALL to Missy to make sure she was all right with keeping Wrigley a little bit longer and stopping by her place to throw on some workout clothes, Mia sat on a stationary bike with Zoe on one side and Brooke on the other.

A young woman with two long, dark braids and way too much energy sat on a bike perched on a rectangular pedestal, facing them. A row of mirrors covered the wall behind her. "I'm so glad you guys are here," she said. "My name is Ashley and I've been a spin instructor for three years. Have any of you taken a class before?"

Zoe and Brooke each raised a hand, making Mia more insecure as she shifted her feet attached to the pedals. "What have I gotten myself into?" she asked with a shaky laugh. The idea of giving Chet some space had prompted her to accept Zoe's invitation, but second thoughts had her yearning to be anywhere but here.

"Don't worry," Ashley said. "I'll make this as painless as possible."

Brooke secured her brown hair in a high ponytail tail then gripped the handles. "I've only taken a couple classes and it was years ago. If you're in pain, I will be too."

Ashley laughed. "I'll take it easy. Zoe mentioned wanting to experience the class, seeing if it'd be a good fit for what ya'll do so I'll do a quick twenty-minute session, giving you a good glimpse into how things usually go. I want to give my students a good workout, but I also aim to give them a place for self- reflection. A time to let out whatever's holding them back."

Mia swallowed hard. Now wasn't the time to self-reflect and let the torrent of emotions inside her loose. But she was literally locked into this now. She had no choice but to get through, hopefully in one piece.

Picking up a little remote, Ashley aimed it at the wall and turned the lights down. Music blasted to life from a speaker mounted in the back of the room.

"Let's get started," Ashley said, her smooth voice coming to life from a microphone hooked on her ear. "Find the beat of the music. Moving your legs, hands on the front of the handlebars."

Mia mimicked Ashley's pose, moving her legs and picking up the pace to match the rhythm beating through the room. Song after song played, the instructor barking out different positions and orders that her body struggled to achieve. The muscles in her legs screamed. Her lungs burned. Sweat poured from her hairline.

What seemed like hours later, Ashley stepped off her bike and brought a handful of electric candles to life, illuminating the dark room. "We've reached our hill, ladies. Standing out of the saddle, I want you to make those wheels sticky."

Mia stood, her feet still attached to the pedals, and turned the small knob on the bike like she'd been taught and groaned. She shifted her weight from one leg to another, using all the energy she had left to push the pedals.

"I want you to think about what hill you're climbing in your life." Ashley swung her leg over her bike, pedaling while standing like the rest of them, but no breathlessness broke up her words. "What do you need to push past? What do you need to conquer to put you on a better path to meet your goals? What's holding you back?"

The words slammed against Mia's chest, making it even harder to push the air from her lungs. At this point in her life, it was easier to ask what wasn't holding her back.

"Now take those thoughts and emotions and fears and doubts and know that you are capable of pushing through anything this world throws your way, just like you're able to push up this hill. That you can accomplish anything."

The positive sentiments mixed with the music and the pain shooting up Mia's legs and shattered the dam holding back all of her emotions for the past few days. Tears dotted her eyes as she struggled to keep the wheels of her bike spinning, to get to the top of the hill. Something inside her urging her to keep moving, keep going, as if getting to the top of this imaginary hill would prove something—even if only to herself.

"You made it to the top," Ashley yelled through the mic. "Now, it's time to speed back down that hill."

Mia's tiny moment of relief was quickly replaced with dread. The slow, steady beat pulsing through the room changed, the tempo becoming faster.

"Go ahead and sit back down. Take off all the resistance on your bike," Ashley commanded. "Once we get down this hill, class is over, so give me everything you have left."

Mia wanted to laugh, but it'd take way too much energy to do anything besides struggle for her next breath. She sat, relieved to take the pressure off her shaky legs. She turned the little knob in the opposite direction and the wheels moved easier. She pedaled to the beat of a song she hadn't heard since high school, nostalgia giving her a little extra motivation to get this stupid class over with.

"When the hook comes on, I want you to grit your teeth and pedal as fast as you possibly can to the finish line."

Mia sucked in a deep breath and mopped the sweat off her brow. The lyrics changed to the familiar chorus, and she moved her legs so fast she was afraid her damn bike might actually charge forward. Closing her eyes, she ignored all the pain engulfing her—pain in her muscles and the pain in her heart. She needed to accomplish her goal today, to see a positive result based on her effort. Something to wipe away even the tiniest smudge of depression from her afternoon.

"You did it!" Ashley let out a whoop of joy. "Slow those legs, ladies. Let your heart rate climb down. Take a second and know that you are amazing."

Amazing? Mia felt more like an out-of-shape woman who'd fall on her face as soon as she stepped off the bike. But she was proud that she'd made it through the class. Even if she may regret it in the morning when she couldn't get out of bed.

After a brief cool down, led by the way-too-perky Ashley, Mia unclicked her spin shoes from the pedals and draped herself over the handlebars. "I don't trust myself to stand yet."

Brooke chuckled. "Same. That was intense."

"Good or bad intense?" Ashley asked, then brought the lights back to full force.

"Ask me tomorrow," Brooke said. "But I liked it. It's a good workout, but it's more than that. You were great at really making me dig deep within myself. To make this a mental exercise as well as a physical one. That's exactly what we like to do at Crossroads Mountain Retreat."

Mia sniffed back tears. So she wasn't the only one who'd been impacted by the encouraging words being barked out by the instructor.

A hand on Mia's shoulder lifted her head. Zoe stood beside her, her cheeks red and wisps of auburn hair dancing around her face. "Are you all right?"

"Why don't I give you all a few minutes to discuss everything," Ashley said. "I'll be in the lobby when you're finished, and we can chat more."

Mia waited for the other woman to leave the room, closing the door behind her, before sitting up straight and wiping her eyes. "I'm fine. I wasn't expecting to get hit in the gut with all these feelings while doing this. I figured I'd be trying not to die." She forced a laugh, but it came out on a choked sob. "I'm sorry. I'm just a little overwhelmed. And then with what happened to Chet earlier, and how he reacted when I touched him."

She squeezed her eyes shut, absorbing the blow that came along with the way Chet had winced when she'd tried to comfort him. At the feeling of rejection at his relief once she'd agreed to go with Zoe and Brooke.

"Oh, honey. You have nothing to apologize for," Zoe said. "You're going through a lot right now. Trust me, I understand. And with Chet..." She shrugged. "You've got to understand how much this weighs on him."

"I do understand. My heart breaks for him. It's just that

the last couple of days has brought us so close, and I could see him rethinking everything. Maybe I should do the same." She'd come to Pine Valley to heal from a broken heart and regain her focus on her dream. Not to get sucked back into a relationship with a man who'd always see her as second best. A man who'd always choose solitude and living in the past over discovering a new future with her.

Brooke swung off her bike and stared at her with large, sad eyes. "I know you have so much whirling around inside you right now. Questions and fear and confusion. But until a few days ago, I hadn't seen Chet smile the way I've seen him smile when he looks at you—haven't heard him laugh. Despite all the bad things that have happened, he's come alive again. You're the reason. Don't give up on him too soon. Don't give up on what you two could be. You bring out something special in each other."

Mia considered her words as she gulped down water from her bottle. She didn't want to give up on Chet, but she also didn't want to waste her time on someone who couldn't give her everything she needed. Everything she deserved. She'd made that mistake once and it'd nearly cost her every-thing. She'd be a fool if she made that same mistake a second time.

18

C het sat on the hard bench nestled off the brick pathway that cut across the grassy square downtown. He kept his gaze glued on Truly's Trading Post, willing Eddy to return from his lunch break. All the steam that had carried him down the hill to town had slowly leaked away, billowing into the afternoon breeze.

A quick glance at his watch told him he'd waited for nearly an hour. Eddy should be back soon. The cashier he'd spoken with when he'd arrived told him he'd just missed Eddy. So he'd found a spot outside, sat, and waited.

And tried to forget the flash of hurt in Mia's eyes when he'd flinched away from her comforting touch.

Running his tongue along the inside of his mouth, he forced the image away. He couldn't get sucked into her vortex anymore. He had to focus on finding the killer and nothing else. Only then would he find some sort of peace in this twisted world. And if he found out that Bobby was the man who'd murdered so many innocent women, including his family, then the world was even more twisted than he'd even realized.

An old red truck with Truly's Trading Post scrawled along the side in white loopy letters turned onto the square and parked in front of the store. Eddy unhooked his seatbelt then twisted to search for something in the back seat.

Chet stood and crossed over the ankle-high grass to meet Eddy. His heart thundered in his chest with each step. His nerves stretched so tight they threatened to snap. Eddy had lied once to protect his uncle. Chet needed to make sure that didn't happen again. Not when the stakes were this damn high.

Chet rapped his knuckles against Eddy's window, his mouth pressed in a firm line.

Eddy jumped, then turned toward him. Relief sagged his shoulders, a frown firmly in place, and his eyes shifted like a child who'd been caught in the wrong—already coming up with excuses.

Instead of stepping out of the truck, Eddy powered down the window. "Hey, man. What's up?"

"You tell me," Chet said, crossing his arms over his chest and ignoring the itching sensation burning rings around his wrists.

Eddy narrowed his gaze. "Excuse me?"

"Don't play dumb. How could you lie to the police about where Bobby is? How could you lie to me? I thought we were friends."

A flash of irritation rippled across Eddy's face, turning his pale skin red. Chuckling, he rubbed the back of his neck. "Friends, huh? Is that why you're always chasing me away? I've tried for years to be your pal. Yours and Tucker's. You've never seemed too interested in that, until now. When you want me to turn my back on my family even though we both know Bobby isn't capable of hurting anyone."

Eddy's answer reared back Chet's head. Sure, Eddy

could be a bit of a pest, but he and Tucker had always included him. Letting him tag along whenever he was in town. But that shouldn't matter. All that mattered was the truth. "Dude, I don't have the time or the patience to dissect whatever the hell type of relationship me and you have. Friendship. Pals. Acquaintances. That's not the point. The point is you lied to cover for Bobby. That doesn't help anyone here. Not even him."

Hanging his head, Eddy gripped the bottom of the steering wheel and sighed. "You're right. I'm sorry. I just got scared, all right? Those bodies showed up on Uncle Bobby's property and he's nowhere to be found. That doesn't look good. I figured if I mentioned he was with Aunt Missy on that cruise, all suspicion of him would blow over so the police could focus on who was responsible. I mean, you don't really think it could be him, do you?" He straightened and locked his weary gaze on Chet.

Chet looked away, unable to meet his eye. "I don't know what I believe anymore." Saying the words out loud made his stomach roll. Bobby had stood by his side, hell had carried him from one day to the next, in his darkest hour. The idea that he could be a serial killer was almost more than he could bear. But he couldn't ignore the facts, and those facts were piling up against Bobby.

"I need to talk to him. Do you have any idea where he could be?"

Eddy shrugged. "I've checked all his normal hunting spots and nothing. Called and there's no answer. I don't know what else to do to get him back here. I know he can clear his name. We just have to find him."

Chet swung his gaze toward the storefront of the trading post. He'd spent countless hours inside with Bobby, buying camping gear and bait for fishing. The older man had been like a father to him when he'd needed one. Had acted like a father when he no longer had a child of his own to look after. That was what had bonded the two of them. That deep loss.

A thought dawned on him. "I didn't know Bobby before Shelly died."

Eddy stiffened, crushing his eyes closed for a moment before opening them again and letting out a deep breath. "He was a different man then. Hell, we were all different before Shelly passed."

A human didn't stumble along the path of grief without it leaving scars. But he wanted specifics. "How so?"

Eddy cocked his head to the side and stared out the windshield, as if glimpsing into the past. "How does any father change when their child is killed? He's a shell of the man he once was. Quieter. More of a loner. Started doing more camping and hunting. Him and Aunt Missy stayed as strong as they could, but something broke that could never be fixed." He caught Chet's eye then winced, as if realized the parallels between Bobby and Chet. "Sorry, man."

Nodding, Chet pushed down the ball of despair that never went away. Now wasn't the time to dwell on his own pain. He understood how Bobby could change, but he didn't fit the image of a loner in Chet's mind. He roamed around town every day with his trusted toolbox, helping anyone in need.

Clearing the emotion from his throat, he focused on Eddy's description of his uncle. "Hard to imagine him more outgoing than he is now. He always has a smile and kind word to offer along with a helping hand. Something inside him might not have mended after Shelly's death, but he must have been a better man to begin with than I ever was," he said, more to himself than to Eddy. "Maybe having a child die at the hands of someone else changes a parent in a different way."

"What do you know about Shelly's death?" Eddy asked, the words slow and cautious.

"Not much," Chet said. "I don't ask questions, and Bobby doesn't talk about it. Always figured if he wanted me to know, he'd tell me."

Eddy's mouth dropped. "So you don't know how she died?"

The question twisted something inside him. "Heard it was an accident of some kind. Bobby found her in the back yard."

"Bobby did find her, but her death wasn't an accident," Eddy said. "Someone killed Shelly, and no one has every figured out who."

MIA STOOD on her porch and lifted a hand to wave as Zoe drove away. Wrigley sat beside her, tail wagging and gazing up at her with big brown eyes. She debated her next move. A shower was a must after her sweaty workout, but the idea of being alone in her apartment in the tub had too many Pyscho-vibes coursing through her mind. Chet's truck was parked in the driveway, so she assumed he was home. She toyed with the idea of knocking on his door to let him know she was back, but the fear of his rejection kept her hands firmly at her sides.

Man, she hated this feeling of helplessness and hopelessness, all packaged neatly together with a bow of anxiety. She pressed a hand to her stomach, praying for some sort of sign to tell her what to do.

The call of a bird lifted her gaze overhead. Long wings

stretched out as a hawk glided along the sky. She wished she could be so free. To just spread her arms wide and ride the wind, letting it carry her away from all her problems. All her worries. But since that would never happen, she needed to come up with an alternative.

Fishing on the dock.

Chet had shared his zen activity with her. At the time, she'd scoffed at the idea, but sitting on the dock and staring at the pond had been peaceful. She could do without the actual fishing, but maybe if she dug out the poles and tackle, Chet would see and join her. Then they might fall into a comfortable silence, forgetting the moment when his reaction to her touch had cut her like a knife.

"What do you think, boy? Should we do some fishing?" She asked Wrigley as she ran her palm over his furry head.

He barked once as if to answer her and stood at attention.

Decision made, she chuckled at her new pup's conversation skills and hurried down the steps. She rounded the cabin, the dog by her side, and made a beeline to the little shed where Chet had stored the fishing gear. The logs of the shed matched the cabin, but the door was a cherry red. She opened it wide and wrinkled her nose at the smell of mildew and dirt. "Guess I can't be afraid to get my hands a little dirty," she said over her shoulder.

She took one step inside and searched for a light switch.

Wrigley stood by the threshold, not venturing any further than the doorway.

"Chicken," she said, although she couldn't blame him for not wanting to come in. She spotted a white string dangling from the ceiling and pulled it. A dull light illuminated the shed. She blinked away the dust catching on her lashes. The space was smaller than she'd expected, the outside giving the illusion the shed would be a longer rectangle. But crudely made wooden shelves outlined the square room.

"Okay," she said, rubbing her palms together. "Where's the fishing gear?"

The floorboards squeaked as she crossed to a line of shelves. The tackle box Chet had used the day before sat on the middle shelf. She grabbed the black handle and hauled it down to the floor. Now she needed the poles. Turning in a circle, she stopped when she spotted two rods propped against the corner. Perfect. She picked up the tackle box and carried it out to the path that led to the dock, then ventured back in the shed for the poles.

As she reached for them, a tiny tapping noise caught her attention. Like the sound of an animal skittering inside the walls after it'd climbed inside to escape the cold. She furrowed her brow, curiosity drawing her closer to the wall. If the woods were on the other side, there was no reason to hear a rodent's claws clacking along a man-made surface— should be no space for a critter to hide.

Pivoting to the side to squeeze her arm between the small space where the two shelving units almost came together, she skimmed her hand against the wall. The smallest amount of pressure caused the old wood to bend.

Weird. The rounded logs that made up the shed were way too sturdy to cave in at all. She dug her phone from her pocket and turned on the flashlight, searching for anything askew. The wall didn't look like it was made of the thick logs, so she shoved a hand behind the shelf and grazed the pads of her fingers against the rough wood. Her finger hooked on a divot, and her heart jumped into her throat.

Saying a quick prayer a squirrel didn't chomp down on

her skin, she pulled her finger back until she heard a tiny *click* and a whoosh of wind leaked through a crack.

What the heck?

Shimmying from her corner, she hurried in front of the shelves bolted to the walls. She quickly moved the clutter to the floor to get a better picture of what lay on the other side. The wall was made of plywood. Once everything was cleared away, a tiny, crudely made door was cracked open— the size no bigger than a breaker box. Sucking in a deep breath, she swung the door open and lifted her phone to illuminate what was inside.

Rolls of thick, black rope like the ones she'd seen hanging from the tree sat inside, and she stumbled backward, her feet not stopping until she raced up the steps of the deck and reached the backdoor to Chet's apartment. She pounded on the door. "Chet! Come quick!"

Wrigley stood beside her, the hairs on his neck at attention as if sensing something wasn't right.

The door burst open, Chet towering over her with a deep frown and worried eyes. "What? What happened? Are you okay?"

She pointed to the shed. "I found rope in the shed. In a secret spot behind the wall."

Without a word, Chet stormed down the stairs and across the yard.

Mia's over-worked legs shook like jelly as she ran after him, fear mounting inside her with each new question her mind formed.

Chet disappeared inside the shed, and she stopped in the doorway. His giant body making the space even more suffocating.

"Look at the wall behind the middle shelf in the back. Where I pulled away all the stuff."

Chet ducked down, pulling out the flashlight of his phone. "Shit. I need to call this in." He reemerged, a world of hurt and confusion knitted on his brow

She brought her shaking hand to her collarbone. Words refused to form into a coherent sentence. But only one word was needed right now. "Bobby."

Chet shoved a hand through his hair. "Doesn't look good."

Disappointment and sadness clashed as loud as thunder across his face. She wanted to comfort him, but his earlier rebuff had her keeping her comments—and her hands—to herself. "Do you really think he's a killer?"

He hung his head, giving it a little shake. "Until we're able to talk to him, I just don't know anymore."

She swished her mouth to her side. She didn't want to sit around and wait for Bobby to be found to solve this. To sit and wait for more threats and acts of violence. An idea took form. "We can't talk to Bobby until we find him, but there is someone else we can talk to."

Chet's eyebrows snapped down above his brown eyes. "Who?"

"Professor Lipton. You were convinced he was the guilty. Maybe he is." All signs might point to Bobby but she struggled to align the man she'd known the last couple months with the monster terrorizing Chet and murdering innocent women. If there was any way someone else could be responsible, she wanted to find them.

He shook his head. "He won't talk to me. Not after I dragged his name through the mud."

She shrugged and beat back the doubt creeping up her spine. She needed to act, to do something, to keep climbing that metaphorical hill. "You can't, but I can."

———

19

C het considered Mia's offer to speak to Professor Lipton as Cruz and Lincoln marched to and from the shed, carrying out evidence bags and lining them on the worn path that led to the dock. He clung to the idea that someone besides Bobby was the guilty party, and all he had to do was prove it. But as the bags mounted higher, his hopes dipped lower.

"I think we've got everything we need." Cruz shoved the blue gloves that had covered his hands in his pocket than dusted his palms off against the thighs of his pants.

Chet surveyed the collection waiting to be processed. Bags of rope along with threads of random material found on the edge of the shelves, as if snagged while shoving things in the hiding spot. Zip ties and duct tape were also confiscated, although those items were placed on the shelves. Left out in the open like the other items in the shed. "What's next?"

Grimacing, Lincoln removed a pair of gloves then rubbed the back of his neck. "Test for prints. Compare what we found in the graves and see if anything is similar. Match the rope. We already know it's more of a specialty product, and that it's sold at Truly's Trading Post. We haven't uncovered any receipts for this rope, but it may have been purchased years ago. That's something I hope we can find out."

"We really need to talk to Bobby," Cruz said, his gaze fixed on the ground.

Mia stood with her arms wrapped around her middle, her new dog laying on the ground in front of her. "What about Missy? She opened up a little bit more when we visited her earlier. Maybe she could shed some light on some of this." She flung a hand toward the evidence then quickly secured her arm back over the other.

Lincoln sighed. "She might not have a choice. I'm going to try to get a warrant. This is damning enough. If we can search Bobby's house and find more circumstantial evidence, we can make a harder push for his location."

The thought of the police combing through Bobby's house without him there, with Missy helpless to do anything but watch and worry, made Chet sick. But he couldn't let his personal feelings get in the way of advancing this investigation. "What's being done now to find Bobby? Do you have officers searching the woods?"

Cruz shook his head. "Nothing beyond popping over to his usual hunting spots and coming up empty. We've asked Eddy for other ideas, but he doesn't have any. Without concrete evidence, we don't have the resources to do a full man hunt. But this might change things."

"What about Grace?" Chet asked. "She's the best tracker in the tri-state area. Has anyone spoken to her about trying to track Bobby?" Now that he thought of it, he kicked himself for not speaking with Grace sooner. As a coworker at Crossroads Mountain Retreat, and a friend, she'd readily offer her services if he asked. Regardless of Cruz and Lincoln's opinion, he made a mental note to contact her when he got a chance.

"I'll speak with her if and when it comes to needing her assistance," Cruz said. "Until now, Bobby is a person of interest rather than a suspect. Shifting how he's labeled will change our approach going forward."

Lincoln scooped a large blue duffle bag with PVPD on the side from the sidewalk and opened it wide. He took the evidence bags and filled the duffle before hooking it on his shoulder. "I want to get started with this. Cruz, can you work on securing the warrant?"

Cruz nodded.

"Thanks for coming so quickly," Mia said, staying glued to her spot on the grass, out of the way. Her words were clipped, as if hurrying them along.

They waved their goodbyes and trudged toward Lincoln's cruiser parked at the front of the house.

Once the Sawyer brothers were out of view, Mia turned to Chet. "All right. How should we do this? If Professor Lipton still has a similar class schedule, he should be on campus for another couple of hours. We could head there now, and I can ask him some questions."

A twinge of trepidation tickled his spine. As much as he relished the thought of getting some answers from the man he'd always pinned as a killer, the idea of placing Mia in a dangerous situation didn't sit right. "I don't know if it's such a good idea."

She dropped her hands to her sides, jaw hanging open. "Why not? You said it yourself, he won't speak with you. And now, the police have their sights set on Bobby even more. Professor Lipton isn't even on their radar. I trust your instincts, and if something told you this man is guilty, that needs to be explored. Who better to do that than me?"

"I can think of plenty of people who'd be better to question a possible suspect," Chet said. "The entire police department for starters. He could be dangerous. If he realizes your intent, he could react poorly. I can't put you in the line of fire."

"You're not putting me anywhere. This is my idea. I want to do this. And if you don't come with me, I'll just go alone." She set her jaw in a look of defiance he'd witnessed countless times in the kitchen. But this time, it didn't irritate the hell out of him.

It scared him.

"Not an option," he said, his wheels spinning as he tried to figure out the best way to handle this. He didn't want to control her like her ex. Hell, he'd all but decided to keep distance between them and not get caught up in all these feelings she stirred. But if she was hellbent on visiting the college to speak with Professor Lipton, he would be as close to her as possible while she did. "Fine. I'll drive you and make sure you're safe. But I don't want you to provoke him."

A nervous smile played on her face. "We'll have a twenty-minute drive to figure out exactly what I should say."

Wrigley barked, drawing their attention.

Mia frown. "What about him?"

Chet groaned. Part of the reason he never wanted to have a dog was figuring out what to do with the damn thing at moments like these. "He'll have to stay here, and we'll have to hope he won't destroy the place. We need to get him supplies, possibly a crate, so we won't have to worry the next time we have to leave him alone."

Mia nodded, and a light blush colored her cheeks.

He blew out a long breath. *We.* He had no right

clumping them together and dictating plans for any kind of future. Even the future of her pet. But he couldn't seem to stop himself. Couldn't control the natural urge to see Mia—and her dog—as a permanent part of his life.

No matter how terrifying the prospect.

A QUICK SEARCH of the community college's current classes showed Mia that Professor Lipton's schedule hadn't changed much. Once Chet parked his truck in the lot next to the business building, she'd have a few minutes to get inside and catch him after class. Although he probably had office hours, it'd be safer for her to speak to him with other students milling around than trapped inside an office.

Chet shifted the car into Park and turned to face her, draping his arm over the back of the bench seat. "Are you sure you're okay with this?"

She filled her lungs with air and fought to keep any signs of nervousness from her voice. If he sensed she was even the least bit hesitant, he'd throw the truck in reverse and hightail it out of there. "Yes. We already went over the best way to approach this. I'll be gone five, ten minutes tops. Nothing bad will happen."

He worked his jaw back and forth. "I'll make sure of that. I'll walk in behind you and stay close. But just in case things don't go as planned..." he flipped open the glove box then pulled out a pocketknife. "Keep this on you."

The sight of the palm-sized weapon tickled her nerves, but she accepted it. The silver was dull and CMB was etched in thin, fancy letters on the front. She brushed the tip of her finger over the indent. "What does that stand for?"

"My initials. It was a gift." He cleared his throat and drew her attention to his face.

He stared out the windshield, his jaw tight, the way it always was when he didn't want to talk. When something upset him, and he was struggling to hold himself together. Yesterday, she would have rested a hand on his and offered to listen to his troubles or throw her arms around him.

Now, they were back to where they started their relationship. Him holding everything in and her too scared of his stinging rebuff to support him. Only now, the ache in her heart made this familiar interaction so much worse.

"Thanks," she said, "I'm sure I won't need it, but I'll feel better knowing it's close." She wasn't just talking about the pocketknife, but this weird energy between them made it impossible to confess all the heavy and confusing emotions pressing down on her chest, stealing her breath.

She tossed the knife in her purse then crossed the strap over her body so the bag rested near her hip on the right side. In easy access if needed. "We should get going."

Her heart sped up as she jumped down from the truck. Chet would stay in the vehicle for a couple minutes then follow her inside. Each step she took put him further behind her, making her nerve endings spark with unease. The late afternoon breeze barreled across the lot, and chills swept up her arms. The thin long-sleeved T-shirt not doing much to shield her.

The sun shifted behind a cloud, casting long shadows over the red brick of the business building. When she reached the glass door, she glanced behind her shoulder. Chet stood outside his truck and gave one nod, encouraging her onward.

Steeling her nerves, she rested one hand on her purse, the knowledge of what lay inside calming her, then stepped through the doorway. She passed the stairs directly to her right and made her way down the wide, familiar hallway. Bright lights bounced off the shiny, linoleum floor. The flood of students flowing from a room at the end of the hall told her where she needed to go.

A sense of nostalgia washed over her. She'd taken classes three days a week for an entire semester. No matter how tired or overworked, she'd been determined to better herself. She made the drive, sat in the class, and absorbed everything she could—forcing her dreams into a reality.

Then her entire life had been derailed.

But not anymore. She was taking control. Starting with talking to Professor Lipton. Then, she'd get her life back on track—full steam ahead.

She reached the door to the classroom as the last of the students trickled out. She sidestepped across the threshold and lightly rapped her knuckles on the door.

Professor Lipton stood in front of the room, swiping away blue marker from a white board hung on the cinderblock wall. His brown hair had thinned at the top, long wisps combed over to hide a small bald spot. But his shoulders were as broad as she remembered, his body fit and strong. "What'd you forget?" He asked, his back to her.

A ball of fear lodged in her throat, and all the questions she had prepared to ask flew out of her head. This was the man Chet was convinced killed his family. Could the police really have missed something when they'd investigated him years before? Could this be the man terrorizing her the last couple days, and did she really believe a simple conversation would give her the answers?

"Well, what is it?" He asked, setting the eraser on a metal lip on the board and turning her way. Wire rimmed glasses circled his owlish eyes and the lines on his forehead were more pronounced than she remembered.

She forced a smile and lifted her hand in an awkward wave. "Hi Professor. Remember me?"

His lips curved up in obvious delight. "Mia! It's been a while. How are you?"

"Fine," she said with a small shrug. "How are you?"

"Oh, the usual. I'm pleased to see you. Are you taking classes again?" He took two steps to the metal desk angled toward the window and gathered a pile of papers into a neat stack.

"Not right now, but I plan to come back soon." At least that part wasn't a lie. She didn't feel the need to earn a degree, but she had more to learn about operating her own business if she wanted to be a success. "I was driving through town and thought I'd stop by. Check in and see if classes were posted yet for next semester."

"Not sure if they're posted, but I know the classes I'm teaching." He dipped down and pulled a sheet of paper from his briefcase. "Have a look if you'd like. I'm teaching a couple of advanced classes that would benefit you. As long as you're still considering opening that restaurant you mentioned."

She took a step forward, then hesitated. Being alone with him in a classroom wasn't much safer than in his office. But the door was wide open, and he'd know something was off if she didn't accept the schedule. Keeping as much distance between them as possible, she accepted the paper and skimmed the list. "I should be able to make this work. Thank you."

"Good," he said, sliding the now-neat stack of papers into his bag. "Is there anything else I can do for you?"

She studied the sheet harder, taking note of the times and days. "Is this the same schedule you're teaching now?"

He shrugged. "More or less. I've cut back a bit since you were here. Each semester I try to cut a little, but it never seems to happen."

"Oh, really? Why's that?" She folded the sheet of paper and slipped it in her pocket. He hadn't offered for her to keep it, but she wanted the exact times he was teaching.

He lifted his hand and pointed to his ring finger. "I got married last year. For the first time in forty-three years, I need to figure out that home, work-life balance everyone's always talking about."

The sight of the gold band around his finger shocked her. "Congratulations."

"If that's all you need, I have to get going," he said, gathering his briefcase in his hand. "I'm glad you stopped by and look forward to seeing you next semester. But the wife's waiting. You know what they say. Happy wife, happy life."

He crossed toward her, and she back peddled out of the room until she connected with hard muscle. Warm breath tickled her neck. *Chet.*

She glanced up into his cold, furious eyes, his gaze locked squarely on Professor Lipton.

"Heard that saying myself," Chet said, his voice raw with anger. "But your wife will have to wait a little bit longer."

20

Chet stepped in front of Mia, putting himself between her and the man who'd haunted his dreams for the last five years. He didn't trust the asshole, no matter what the police said. Not after the way he'd treated Laurie, a student who shouldn't have had to worry about being hit on by a teacher. Not after he'd made advance after advance on his wife. And definitely not when he was the last person to see his wife and daughter alive.

Professor Lipton's face morphed into an angry shade of red, and he bounced his gaze from Chet to Mia. "Do you know this man, Mia?"

The sound of his voice made Chet's blood burn. "Don't talk to her. Don't even look at her." He all but spat out the words. Damnit, he shouldn't have brought Mia here. Shouldn't have agreed to her plan. But even the slightest chance of putting an end to this nightmare, of proving Bobby wasn't involved in any way, had pushed him to behave recklessly.

Sighing, Professor Lipton set his briefcase on the floor by his side and lifted his palms in the air. "We're not doing this again. How many times do I have to tell you I'm sorry about Laurie—"

"Don't you dare say her name."

Mia flattened her hand against the small of his back and his tightened muscles loosened a fraction.

She stepped to his side, her hand still pressed against him. "Chet is my coworker."

He flinched at the casual description of their relationship. What the hell was wrong with him? He finally stood face-to-face with the man he believed for so long had stolen everything from him, had tied him up and left him for dead, and he was more concerned with the label Mia slapped on him.

Confusion knitted Professor Lipton's brow. "I don't understand. You came together? Why? What do you want from me?"

"The truth," Chet barked. "For once and for all. Confess what you did and put this whole thing to rest."

Deflating, Professor Lipton pinched the bridge of his nose. "How many times do we have to rehash this? The only thing I'm guilty of is being too friendly with one of my students. I regret that now, I really do. I misread Laurie's friendliness and wanted to pursue something that wasn't there. Something I had no right to. I apologize for that. But that doesn't make me guilty of murder. I told you and the police the same damn thing. Hell, I told them again when they called the other day."

"Wait," Chet said, taking a step forward. "You spoke with the police the other day?"

"Yes. I was called about Ms. Simpson." Frowning, he dropped his arm to his side and balled his hand into a fist. "Listen, I get how it raised a red flag. Laurie and Janie were both students of mine. But coincidences happen all the time."

"What about Mia?" Chet studied the man's face, searching for any indication he was hiding something.

"What about her?" Professor Lipton asked, his bushy brows snapping down low, eyes narrowed.

"She was a student, too." Chet countered. He wasn't willing to give away any more information, but he wanted to see the man's reaction.

The professor threw his hands in the air and a frustrated grunt huffed from his mouth. "So were countless other women. And I've never hurt a damn one. Now if you'll excuse me." He took a step forward, but Chet refused to budge. "My wife will worry if I'm not home in time for dinner. Please. Step aside."

"Why should you be allowed to go home to enjoy a nice dinner with your wife? Does she know how you pressured Laurie? How you lured her to your office time and time again, only to proposition a married woman? You don't deserve love and happiness. You don't deserve a warm meal and a good woman."

"Chet," Mia, said quietly. "Maybe we should go."

Professor Lipton let his head fall forward for a few beats before lifting it again to meet Chet's stare straight on. "I was an asshole. I disrespected your wife and your marriage. I'm sorry for that. But you're wasting your time and your anger on me. I'm not the one you're looking for."

Mia slid a piece of paper from the front pocket of her jeans and unfolded it. She skimmed a finger along the front. "You said your schedule this semester is similar to what is planned for the next one."

He nodded. "Day classes are the same. I dropped an evening class so I can be home."

"So you taught a class yesterday morning?" She asked.

"Two. One at 9:00 am. Another directly after. Then office hours after lunch."

"Then he couldn't have been at the kennel yesterday." Mia slid her hand in Chet's, and the feel of her skin against his was like a soothing balm he didn't know he needed. Damnit to hell, this woman who stood beside him after seeing him at his worst, keeping him grounded, had gotten under his skin in a way he never imagined possible.

"Kennel?" Professor Lipton asked. "Like a dog kennel? Why would I be there? And I still don't understand what any of this has to do with you, Mia."

Chet ignored the questions. "Can someone from your classes vouch you were here?"

Irritation clouded his face, but he nodded. "If it will end this nonsense, I'll get a number of students to verify I was here all morning. I'll give them your information to contact you."

"Just one is fine," Mia said. "Thank you for speaking with us." She tugged at Chet's hand, leading him toward the door.

A crushing blow of defeat slammed against Chet's chest as he turned his back on Professor Lipton and the last chance to prove Bobby's innocence. He'd clung to the desperate need for this man to be guilty so that the one he loved like a father could escape the scrutiny coming his way.

Because if a man he trusted so damn much was a murderer, Chet couldn't handle the earth-shattering blow.

"Chet."

The sound of his name stopped him in his tracks. He turned back around, his stomach revolting against the truth he'd been forced to swallow. Any response clogged in his tight throat, so he simply quirked one brow.

"I don't know a lot about life, but I do know things can get the better if you let them," Professor Lipton said. "Don't let the pain of the past keep you from embracing a new future. You can only swim in your anger and hate for so long before you drown." He aimed a small smile at Mia.

He stared, open mouthed, the wisdom of the words raining down on him. He'd been hesitant to come here today, but he'd gained more than he'd imagined. He'd gained two truths that his soul had needed to learn.

The pain of one might bring him to his knees, and the promise of the other might just give him everything he'd never believed he'd have again.

MIA LEFT Chet sitting in the truck, talking on the phone to Cruz about what had transpired at the college, as she hurried up the walkway to her door. The sun sat low, lighting the sky in subtle shades of orange and pink. The earlier encounter had shaken her in multiple ways and left her with even more questions. Questions about the killer, and questions about her feelings for Chet—and his for her.

But before she could dive into any of that, she had to find out what kind of damage waited for her from Wrigley.

"All right," she said to herself as she unlocked the door and pushed it open. "Here goes nothing."

Wrigley bounded forward, tail wagging and tongue hanging from his wide-open mouth. He lifted his paws and rested them on her chest.

Laughing, she pushed him down. "I missed you, too, but you can't jump. Now let's look and see if you got into any trouble."

She didn't smell anything and prayed that meant he

hadn't made any messes in the house. They hadn't been gone too long, but that didn't mean he hadn't had to relieve himself. She studied the floor with each step, but no puddles waited to be cleaned. "Looks like you were a good boy."

Wrigley stood in front of her, shaking his butt in excitement.

"Now let's check the bedroom." She passed the living room and ducked into the bedroom. Dirty clothes from her hamper where strewn over the floor, a hole in her favorite pair of leggings. With her fists planted on her hips, she faced the dog, who lowered his head and cowered in the corner.

She shook her head, too soft-hearted to do anything more than wag her finger at him. "Bad dog. You can't chew my clothes, or we'll have some real problems." She rubbed his head then gathered the clothes and piled them on a chair.

"Mia?" Chet's voice boomed through the apartment.

"Back here," she called.

Heavy footsteps proceeded Chet down the hall.

Wrigley jumped to his feet and stared at the door.

Chet stopped at the doorway, leaning against the frame and tucking his thumbs into the pockets of his jeans. "How'd he do?" he asked, dipped his chin toward the dog.

Wrigley rushed him and leaned against his legs, demanding Chet's attention.

"Pretty good. No accidents, but my dirty clothes piqued his curiosity a little too much. I should have made sure the door was closed before I left. I feel like I set him up for failure. No toys to chew on. Nothing to keep him busy while he waited."

"We'll head into town first thing in the morning and get everything he needs." Chet chuckled then studied her room.

Heat crept up the back of her neck. He'd never seen her bedroom, and there was something oddly intimate about him in her private sanctuary. Needing to stop thinking about how much she liked him in her room, she blurted out the first thing that came to mind. "Is Cruz mad we went to see Professor Lipton?"

The side of his mouth ticked up at one corner, as if fighting off amusement. "Not too mad."

She waited for him to elaborate but wasn't surprised when he didn't. "And how are you?" She held her breath. The whole ride home she'd kept her questions to herself, not wanting to upset him, but she'd explode if she didn't ask now.

He dropped his head. "I'm not sure. I wanted it to be him."

Her heart twisted at his words, the brokenness of his tone. "So did I."

Lifting his head, he met her stare. "Thank you."

She lifted a shoulder. "I didn't do much."

"You've done everything. And not just today. You've..." he lifted his hands then let them fall to his sides as his voice trailed away. "I don't know what to say or how to say it. Don't know how to make sense of the way you make me feel let alone explain to you. Damnit, I'm not good at this stuff."

Warm appreciation burrowed into the pit of her stomach, arching outward until she practically glowed. "You're better than you give yourself credit for."

"I wasn't earlier." Frowning, he stepped further into her small room. "When I found that teddy bear. It wasn't fair to treat you the way I did. I had so many emotions stirring around. Fear, guilt, sadness. I just wanted space. To be left alone."

She offered him a sad smile. "That's understandable, but I appreciate the apology."

"There's never a good reason for hurting someone you care for. And that's what I did. I saw it in your eyes."

Sensing he needed more than just her reassurances to comfort him, she met him in the center of the room and took both his hands in hers. He towered over her. His size, once so intimidating, now gave her a sense of peace. "Just because you hurt me doesn't mean I didn't understand why it happened. We'll do better next time."

He cut his gaze to the floor. "I don't know if there can be a next time. I don't want to keep hurting you."

She pulled in a deep breath, ready to lay her cards on the table. They'd both been through the ringer, her heart barely healed after Aaron destroyed it, but there was one thing she was certain of. She wanted Chet in her life. And not just as a coworker. If he was part of her big picture—part of her dream of a happy future—she needed to be the one to take the first step. The one to lay her soul bare for this man who stood in front of her. A giant in form but a pile of marshmallow fluff on the inside who was so afraid of losing everything again.

"Keeping your distance because you don't want to hurt me will hurt," she said. "Choosing to protect me by ending whatever we've started isn't a choice I want you to make. I want you, Chet. I want you in any way you're ready to give me."

His head snapped up, eyes wide and filled with tears. "I have so much baggage. I can't ask you to take that on."

She squeezed his hands. "Laurie and Riley and the love you shared with them isn't baggage. It's a beautiful story that I want you to share with me. A beautiful part of your soul I'm honored to know, and that makes you who you are."

He sniffed, lowering his forehead to rest on hers. "Do you know how damn special you are?"

"No, but I don't mind hearing you explain it to me."

He barked out a laugh then gathered her in his arms, holding her close. "I'll tell you every single day if you want."

His words melted something inside, thawed the last piece of her heart that was frozen with Aaron's betrayal. The future might be unclear, but she wanted it to include Chet.

Wrigley barked then whined, spinning in a circle.

She laughed. "I think he needs to go outside."

"You take care of that, and I'll start dinner," Chet said. "Just don't venture far from the cabin."

The simple pleasure of the arrangement, as well as his concern, had her pressing a kiss to his cheek. She could almost believe all their troubles were behind them and this is what life could be like every day.

But the back of her mind warned her not to get too comfortable. A killer still lurked, and once he was found, his real identity might destroy everything she'd built with Chet.

21

C het stacked the logs in the fireplace in Mia's living room then struck a match, sending it onto the kindling. A sense of pride puffed his chest as he watched the flames dance. No matter how many times he built a fire, he never tired of seeing the results burst to life.

"I don't think I've had a fire since I moved in." Mia bustled around the kitchen and cleaned up the dishes from dinner.

"Not surprised," he said, standing and watching her stretch to place a plate in the cupboard. A sliver of skin appeared above the waistband of her pants and the muscles in his stomach tightened.

After the intense conversation they'd shared after arriving home, dinner had been light and airy. Talking about Wrigley and classes Mia wanted to take soon. Steering clear of discussing the nightmare consuming them, the blanket of fear they couldn't shed or the constant barrage of emotions that beat against them like waves on a rocky shore.

Mia wiped her hands on a dish towel then draped it over the counter's edge. "Thanks for dinner."

"No problem. Least I can do." He wanted to do more—to show her how much she meant to him but moving too fast made his head spin. He'd never loved another woman besides his wife.

All the air fled his lungs. Love? It'd only been a handful of days since his guard had been forced down and he'd admitted to himself how much Mia meant to him. But love?

"What's that look for?" Mia stared at him from across the room, a half-filled wine glass in her hand.

He shook his head, smiling as the idea took hold. He might not be all the way there yet, but he was close enough. But he couldn't tell Mia that or he'd scare the shit out of her. "Nothing. Just think I might try some of that wine you love so much."

Brows raised, she tilted her head to the side far enough to cause her long, dark curls to spill over her shoulder. "Really?"

He shrugged, not wanting to admit he'd rather run to his place and grab a beer. "Sure."

"Okay. One glass of merlot coming up." She grabbed a stemless wineglass from the cabinet then scooted the bottle from the counter. She filled his glass, topped off hers, then carried them both to him.

He accepted the wine and took a sip then wrinkled his nose. "Interesting."

She laughed. "You don't have to drink it."

"It's fine," he said, then took her hand and led her to the couch, coaxing her to sit at the far end.

Wrigley spun in a circle by the fire then nestled onto a blanket Mia had laid on the floor for him to sleep on.

Chet set his glass on the coffee table and lowered himself on the end of the sofa.

Mia frowned. "Why so far?"

He chuckled. "This sofa is so small I'm surprised it doesn't snap in two under me. No two people who sit on it are far from each other."

She struggled not to grin. "You know what I mean."

He snagged her bare foot and swung it over to rest on his lap. He folded his hands over the smooth skin and kneaded the pads of his thumbs into her arches. "If you sit too close, I can't do this."

"Oh, God," she said, closing her eyes. "First you cook me dinner. Then a fire with wine and a foot rub? What did I do to deserve all this?"

He took a second to study the slight curves of her face, the delicate slope of her slender neck, and appreciate just how damn beautiful she was. He'd fought his growing attraction to her for months now. Taking the time to observe what made her so alluring felt like a luxury he never thought he'd experience. "How are you doing?"

Her eyes fluttered open, and she lifted one side of her mouth. "Fine. I know this has been horrible for you—"

He halted the motion of his hands on her foot. "No. I don't want to talk about my past or my feelings. I've done enough of that lately, and I want to hear about you. And don't say you're okay because we both know that's bullshit."

She furrowed her brow, causing thin wrinkles to ripple across her forehead. "You want me to unload on you? Are you feeling okay?"

He squeezed her foot then continued giving her a massage, but he couldn't stop the pang of guilt at her astonishment that he actually wanted to hear about how she was handling a stressful situation. "I want to hear it all. Want you to know I'm here for you just like you've been there for me."

"Okay." She sucked in a deep breath then took a long sip

of wine. "Honestly, it's been easier to focus on you. When I stop and consider how I'm holding up, everything that's happened comes crashing down on me and this sense of panic takes hold of my whole body."

"I understand," he said, switching his hands to her other foot. "I suffer from panic attacks. They're no fun."

"How'd you get over them?"

He gave a little self-deprecating laugh. "I didn't. I hid. I refused to talk to anyone. I suffered in silence. All the things I shouldn't have done. Ignoring your anxiety doesn't make it go away."

"I don't think anything will make it go away until the killer is caught." She shivered then stole another sip of wine before setting her drink back on the coffee table. "Then there's this other part of me. The part that's happy this whole mess brought us together—showed me who you really are and how much I care about you. Which, of course makes me feel guilty. I mean, what kind of a person finds joy when there's so much chaos and turmoil surrounding them?" She shifted her lips to the side and tears hovered over her dark lashes.

"A lucky one." Abandoning her foot, he took hold of her hands and pulled her forward, anchoring her in his arms. The feel of her brought parts of him to life he thought long dead. "Life moves on, and we can either find reasons to move with it or stand still in our grief. I've stood still for too long."

"You don't think I'm a bad person for somehow being happy right now?"

He hooked a piece of hair behind her ear then cradled her delicate jaw in his palm. "You're one of the best people I've ever met."

A wobbly smile lifted her lips. "You're not mad at Brooke any more for hiring me?"

"Fortunately, I have strong women around me who know what I need before I do."

She laughed, and the sound expanded his chest. He hadn't had much laughter in his life, and he'd do whatever he could to hear it every damn day.

"And don't you dare forget it," she said, smoothing a hand over his cheek then pressing her lips to his.

The feel of her mouth on his made his heart race. He deepened the kiss, needing to explore her—taste her. She shifted to straddle him, and he brought his hands to meet at the small of her back. The heat of her body engulfed him, desire bursting hotter than the flames dancing in the hearth. His tongue parted her lips and the taste of wine and a hint of mint tickled his senses.

She pulled away, her face hot and her breaths coming in quick, ragged bursts. "You're pretty amazing, Chet, and you're right. I am lucky. Lucky to be here with you."

He wanted to swing her into his arms and carry her to her room to finish what they'd started, but it was too soon. Too fast. Too much to handle on top of the spiral of new emotions making him soar. "Is it okay if we do it again?"

She grinned and leaned down, her mouth hovering just above his. "You can kiss me any time you want."

Entwining his fingers into the hair at the nape of her neck, he captured her mouth once again. Tonight, he'd savor every single second of this woman, then he'd do the same thing tomorrow and the day after for as long as she kept him around.

～

THE SOUND of whining lifted Mia's eyelids, and she came face to face with Wrigley. Yawning, she turned on her side then paused, confused by where she was.

A strong arm latched around her waist, securing her to a hard chest.

Excitement tingled in her tummy, and she raised her chin to stare into Chet's large, brown eyes. "Good morning," she said, unable to hide the smile spreading her mouth wide. Last night had been perfect. Fire, wine, and a night spent on the couch after a hot make-out session.

The side of his mouth hitched up. "Morning."

"How'd you sleep?" She'd slept like a rock, but the couch barely fit his frame. Not to mention she'd slept cuddled against him all night.

"Well, my arm's either asleep or it fell off, and I had a beautiful woman on top of me. How do you think I slept?"

Laughing, she slapped at his chest.

He trapped his hand on top of hers, pinning it against his muscles. All traces of amusement left his face. "I haven't slept so soundly in years."

Heat crashed against her cheeks. "Same."

Wrigley whined again, stealing her attention.

"I need to take him outside." She pushed herself to her feet and ran a hand over her mop of hair.

Chet snagged her hand and yanked her back down then kissed her. "Okay. Now you can go." His phone rang and he sat and reached for it. "It's Cruz. I'm going to take this."

"Let's go Wrigley." She slipped her feet into her sneakers by the door and shrugged into a light jacket. The sun was just bursting through the darkness so the air would still have a bite of chill she didn't want to battle.

Wrigley bounded through the door and ran down the porch steps to the front yard. Drops of dew dotted the green blades of grass, and the blanket of thick clouds swirling in the sky announced more rain to come. But Mia couldn't bring herself to care. Rain or shine, nothing would dampen her day.

When the dog was done sniffing around, he ran back to the porch. She ruffled the fur on the top of his head then headed back inside.

Chet paced across her small living room, the phone pressed to his ear. A frown pulled down his mouth and he nodded before he said goodbye and hung up. "Cruz wanted to give me a heads up the warrant for Bobby's house will probably come through this morning. I want to be available for Missy. The Trading Post will be open in thirty minutes. We should get ready and head into town so we can grab essentials for Wrigley. That way we can have what he needs for a few hours alone in case Missy needs us."

The reality of what waited for them outside of the comforting cocoon of her home crashed down on her like a bucket of icy water, but she wouldn't let it ruin the thrill of happiness humming inside her. As much as the idea of Bobby being a serial killer turned her stomach, the police searching his house could bring an end to this nightmare. Then she and Chet could focus on the relationship blooming between them. "Sounds good. I'll put on the coffee then throw some clothes on."

"You okay if I run over to my place really quick to change? I can wait for you if you'd like."

"Don't be silly. I've got Wrigley. Go. Get ready. Then we'll head into town."

He dipped his chin in acknowledgment then she watched him leave, the hum dimming a little at being alone.

. . .

TWENTY MINUTES LATER, Chet parked his truck in an empty spot outside Truly's Trading Post, right beside the company vehicle. "Looks like Eddy's here. They don't open for another ten minutes, but maybe he'll let us in if we knock," Mia said, unfastening her seatbelt. She hooked her purse across her body.

"Might as well try." Chet hurried out the door then rounded the truck to help her down.

The touch of his hand caused flutters of anticipation to erupt in her stomach. She held on tight as they walked to the locked, glass door and Chet knocked with his free hand.

A few seconds passed before Eddy approached the other side of the door with his eyebrows pulled low. He wore a forest green apron with the company's logo embroidered on the chest over a long-sleeved t-shirt and jeans. Frowning, he unlocked the dead bolt and opened the door. "Hey, you two. What's going on?"

"I need to get supplies for a puppy," Mia said, forcing a cheerfulness to her voice she didn't feel. "I know you aren't open yet, but do you mind if we grab what we need now? We have a busy day, and I don't want Wrigley to go without essentials."

Eddy scrunched his nose. "Wrigley?"

"The dog," Chet said. He stood with his feet hip width apart and scowled. "We need a crate and maybe some toys. Can you help us out?"

Eddy nodded then stepped to the side. "Sure, man. Come on in. I'll show you where the pet supplies are."

Chet pressed a hand to the small of her back and ushered her inside, following Eddy into the quiet store. Music that normally flowed through the speakers hadn't even been turned on yet. The buzz of the lights overhead as loud as a mosquito in her ear.

Eddy turned down a wide aisle and stopped toward the back of the store. "I don't have a ton, but it should be enough to get you and your dog started. Crates, dishes, a few toys."

"Great. Thanks." She crouched and shifted through a container with chew toys that would hopefully keep Wrigley away from her dirty clothes.

A vibration sounded in Chet's pocket, and he plucked out his phone, glancing at the screen before accepting the call. "Hey, Cruz. Did it come through?"

Staying low, she stared up to study Chet's face. Annoyance had him raking a hand over his beard.

"Hello?" Chet said into the phone. "Damnit, the reception's horrible in here."

Eddy shrugged. "Sorry."

"Wait, so you did get the warrant?" Chet took a step backward, as if moving would make the reception better. He spun around, the muscles in his broad back tightening under his red, flannel shirt.

"What's going on?" Eddy asked.

She stood, training her ears to listen to any tidbits from Chet's conversation, but all she heard was him getting more agitated by the poor connection. "I'm not sure." It wasn't a lie, but she didn't think it was wise to say more about what was happening with Eddy's uncle.

Chet spun back around. "I'm stepping outside really quick. Grab what you need, and I'll meet you at the cash register."

"Okay." She forced a tight smile then studied the limited items on the shelf. "I need a crate but the ones you have aren't big enough. Do you have any more?"

"I should," Eddy said. "Come on back and we'll check."

She followed him into the storage room, her mind spinning. If the warrant had come through, Cruz could either be calling to let Chet know he was on his way to Bobby's residence, or he could have started the search and found something of importance. She needed to be there for him in case Cruz had a bomb to drop.

Eddy disappeared behind a wall. "I don't sell a lot of pet supplies," he called out. "I keep stuff I don't sell a lot of back here. Out of the way."

Quickening her pace, she followed his voice and rounded the corner. "I appreciate the help. Sorry if I'm a bother."

Eddy stood with a gun pointed at her chest. "No bother at all. As long as you keep your mouth shut and come with me."

22

The first sprinkles of another damn rainstorm fell from the gray sky as Chet stepped onto the sidewalk. He hunched over his phone, blocking it from getting wet. With the way his luck was going, one drop of water would destroy the ancient device—taking away the voicemails he cherished so much.

"Cruz? Are you still there?"

"Yes, did you hear what I said?"

"No," Chet growled. "Reception was spotty. What's going on? Did you secure the warrant?"

"Yes. Missy's a mess. One of the hardest parts about working in a small town is knowing everyone a little too well. Especially when the job is to comb through their personal belongings looking for evidence."

The revelation straightened Chet's spine and thick drops of water slid down his face into his beard. "You're already there?"

"Warrant came through right after we spoke earlier. I was already down at the station, so didn't take long to make it over here." The tightness of his voice told Chet more than Cruz's words.

"You found something." Chet clenched his jaw, preparing himself for the blow. No matter how he'd told himself over and over to wrap his mind around what the evidence pointed to, hearing the truth about Bobby would be impossible to bear.

But he would do it. He'd lived through worse, and now, he had Mia by his side to help him navigate the betrayal and sadness that was surely to follow.

"We did," Cruz confirmed.

Chet squeezed his eyes closed against the sharp pain piercing through him. "Just tell me."

"We found a little door cut into the wall behind the bed in the guest room. Similar to the one Mia found in the shed at the cabin. There was an old shoebox shoved inside."

Chet held his breath as distress pressed against his lungs. "What was in the shoebox?"

"Sketches of what appear to be different variations of the brand used on all the victims. On you." Cruz's voice dipped low, anger tainting his words.

The brand Chet always covered burned beneath his shirt. He slid his hand up the sleeve and brushed the pad of his thumb over the raised skin.

"That's not all. There were two pictures. One of Laurie when she was a teenager."

"What?" Fury pounded through his veins. Bobby had kept his identity as a murderer well under wraps, but the truth that he'd held a flame or some sick obsession for Laurie since she was a teenager was the shit icing on the fucking cake.

Chet's legs shook and he lowered himself on the edge of

the sidewalk, his feet planted on the side of the road. Moisture seeped into the back of his jeans, but he couldn't care less as his world crashed in around him. "How could I have missed this? How could I not see the type of man Bobby really was?"

"There was another picture," Cruz said, cutting into Chet's ramblings. "One of you, Tucker, and Eddy."

Chet's mouth fell open and his mind spun. "The three of us? Together? From how long ago?"

"Looks like young teens. Eddy has a bandage wrapped around his forearm. You remember when that happened?"

He ran a hand over his face, threading his fingers through his thick beard. "Actually, yeah. Probably the summer he was attacked by a dog. He claimed the neighbor's dog jumped out from the bushes and just latched onto his arm. I always doubted his story because the pet was always docile. But the dog ended up dead, and Eddy's been weird around dogs since."

A flash of clarity parted through the fog of pain engulfing Chet. "Wait a second. Eddy always stayed in the guest room when he crashed with Bobby and Missy, which was pretty frequently. His parents weren't the greatest, and Bobby treated him like one of his own."

"Does Eddy ever stay at the house still?"

Chet shook his head. "I don't know. You could ask Missy."

A memory crashed against Chet, and he shot to his feet. "Shit. Otto."

"Otto? Tucker's dog? What about him?"

He scrambled to his feet and bolted toward the store. He had to get to Mia. He'd left her inside with a killer. The sky opened and the drops of rain came down in torrents. "When Otto saw Eddy the other day at my place, he sniffed him real good. Made Eddy uncomfortable as hell. I figured it was because of his past, but Otto was tracking the killer's scent in the woods. He smelled Eddy."

Chet ran through the downpour and pushed open the door. "Mia!" Nothing but the buzz of electricity in an empty store returned his call.

"Is Mia okay? Where are you?"

Realization almost choked him, blocking his airway. He had to get to Mia. He raced down the aisle to where he'd left her with Eddy, but no one was there. "Mia!" he called again, his heart racing so fast it made him dizzy. "Damnit, she's not here."

"Where?" Cruz shouted, slicing through the furious thoughts and fears running rampant in Chet's mind.

"Truly's Trading Post. Eddy was showing her supplies for her new dog, and I stepped outside to take your call. They're not here." Panic clawed up his throat, and the scars around his wrists burned.

"Check the back," Cruz suggested. The words came out choppy, the syllables shot through the line in cut-off bits and pieces.

Chet sprinted toward the storage room, pounding open the swinging door, only to be greeted by more silence. A clap of thunder echoed off the aluminum roof but sounded close. Too close. He followed the noise, the phone still pressed to his ear. "Shit. The door's open. Two sets of footprints are leading into the back lot. She's gone."

BRANCHES WHIPPED against Mia's face as she sat pinned in front of Eddy, his arms trapping her as he drove a four-wheeler through the woods. The chilly breeze beat back her hair. Her dark ends whipping around. Terror squeezed her throat, and she wanted nothing more than to close her eyes and imagine herself back in her home, tucked safely against Chet's side.

But she couldn't close her eyes. Not when she needed to pay close attention to where Eddy was taking her. The gun wasn't pressed against her back anymore, but no way she could duck under his arms as they flew over the uneven terrain and throw herself from the speeding recreational vehicle. Her teeth rattled, and rain splattered through the canopy of leaves, soaking through her clothes.

The weight of her purse sat on her lap. In his haste to get her onto the four-wheeler Eddy had parked deep in the woods, he hadn't thought to make her leave it behind. Her fingers itched to grab the pocketknife still inside from the day before, but she couldn't risk it. Not now when one wrong move could send her flying into a tree.

A sharp turn on the moss-covered trail had her nearly spilling over the side, and she stifled a scream. Loose stones skittered down a steep ravine.

Eddy squeezed his arms against her sides, keeping her in her seat but causing her skin to crawl from his touch.

Bile crept up her throat and coated her tongue. She forced it back down, keeping her focus on her surroundings. She didn't know the area well, but if she hoped to make it out of this alive, she'd have to find a place to run. To escape. To hide. Chet would know who took her, it was just a question of how long it'd take for him to discover her gone and if he could find her before it was too late.

Minutes ticked by and the hill steepened. The engine revved as the climb continued. A break in the trees to her right caught her attention. She squinted through the thickening rain and the outstretched branches blocking her view. She sucked in a sharp breath. They were passing the pond behind her cabin. Surely, he wasn't taking her back to her apartment. If so, she just might stand a chance against him.

A swift turn to the left told her she wasn't so lucky. Minutes ticked by, the wheels of the four-wheeler slowing in the slick mud of the path. The distinct smell of a campfire reached her nose and tightened her already rigid muscles. The familiar scent from when Eddy had pressed her against him in the kennel the day before assaulted her senses.

"Almost there," he whispered in her ear, his hot breath making her cringe. "Then the real fun can begin."

She searched through the thicket for the fire. Why had he left a fire burning when he'd planned to be in town working all day? And how was it still going in the rain?

The thick branches thinned, the trees clearing. Wisps of smoke spiraled into the sky. A circular patch of grass surrounded a giant oak tree. Stones encased a fire, a long patch of material stretched over top it, hanging from a nearby maple with thick, black rope.

Behind the fire was a what looked like an old wooden fort. Crudely cut out windows on either side of a door were covered from the inside with dirty cloth. The flat roof was no taller than six feet high, the width of the space about the size of her modest bedroom.

Eddy parked the four-wheeler beside the fire and stepped off, grabbing her arm and forcing her down to meet him.

She glanced behind her, searching for another glimpse of her home. But only upturned roots and the blossoms of spring surrounded her.

But the cabin was just beyond. Just out of sight. Just out of reach.

How many times had Eddy sat in this creepy hideout

and stared through the forest, knowing she and Chet were right on the other side?

A shiver ripped up her spine.

"Sit by the fire," Eddy said, forcing her under the tarp. He kept a firm grip on her arm. "It'll warm you up."

Rain dripped down her face and she dragged her feet as she did what he demanded. As much as she wanted to be obstinate, being numb with cold wouldn't help her. With her hand on her purse, she knelt next to the fire.

Eddy settled beside her, the gun back in his hands and pointed at her ribs.

"What do you want with me?" She asked, a tremor of fear shaking her vocal cords. The not-too-long ride here had made it impossible to do anything but keep her mouth shut and her eyes open.

He smirked. "You're the final blade that will take Chet down."

His words shocked her, and she gave a little shake of her head as if it'd help her understand. "Chet? I thought you were friends?"

"Friends?" Eddy snorted. "I was always just the annoying pest who got in the way. Never allowed to get too close. Never allowed to get what I wanted. He got the girl, got Bobby, got everything that should have been mine."

Her mind struggled to keep up. Each sentence more confusing than the last. The sounds of rain hitting the tarp overhead assaulted her ears. "How could Chet take anything from you?"

A flash of anger contorted Eddy's face. "Laurie was the only one who was kind to me, but she fell for his oafish charm. Married him instead. Uncle Bobby always wanted a son, and when I figured out how to have him for myself—to take Shelly out of the picture, he broke. Pushed me aside, only to be a father again when Chet needed him. Looking past me and my needs just like everyone always has."

Her stomach rebelled. Was Eddy saying he'd started this entire descent into death and destruction to win over the affections of others? Like a child falling on the floor and throwing a tantrum to get a toy from a frazzled adult.

But Eddy had resorted to much worse than a temper tantrum. He'd murdered innocent women. Took the life of a child. And if she understood him correctly, killed his young cousin for the love an uncle.

She couldn't help but wonder why. And if she could get him talking, she could buy herself some time. "Why did you need Bobby's attention? What about your own father?"

"My father never wanted a damn thing to do with me." He picked up a long metal poker from the ground and stuck the end in the fire. The circular tip burned red, making the intricate swoops of a design she'd seen before glow.

Oh my God. The brand.

The contents of her stomach shot to the back of her throat. She scrambled onto her knees and retched into the high grass that stood outside the door of the little fort.

Eddy laughed, loud and cruel, and yanked hard on her hair, lifting her chin to the fat raindrops. "Don't go too far. I have plans for you."

She didn't want to know what was to come, but if she had a clue as to what she was up against, she could figure out how to fight back. "What? You're going to burn that mark into my skin then kill me and bury me in a shallow grave like all the other women? How original."

Keeping his grip on her long strands, he crouched low, pressing his mouth close to her cheek. "Don't worry. That's not all I'll do."

She shifted her gaze to the ground. He'd tossed the

poker to grab her hair. If she could reach the end of it, she stood a chance of hitting him with it and running away. All she had to do was slam it against him hard enough to shock him for a second.

A wet cough from inside the fort reached her ears and her heart stopped. She shot her gaze to the door.

"Uncle Bobby must be waking up. Perfect. I thought everything might be ruined when I had to act quicky back at the store. But now that you're both here, I can make this work. I'll find a way to pin everything on him."

Hope crashed to the muddy ground. If Bobby was in the fort, she couldn't leave him in Eddy's clutches.

Which meant when she got her opportunity, she'd have to do more than hurt him. She'd have to kill him.

23

The rain continued in sheets, washing away whatever tracks etched the woods. Chet kicked a pile of stones in the empty lot behind the trading post. Anger boiled in his gut, ready to explode any minute. Panic gripped his chest, and the urge to scream out his fury clawed at his throat. "We're wasting time. Eddy had to have taken her through the woods. His damn truck is still parked out front. We need to go after them."

Tucker ran a hand over his face. "We can't just go charging into the wet forest with the rain coming down harder by the second." He kept an eye on Otto who trained his nose to the wet ground at the tree line.

Chet had called Tucker as soon as he'd hung up with Cruz. Tucker had wasted no time getting into town. Now the two of them, along with Otto, scoured the overgrown weeds and tangles of brush and grass behind the store. No foot-prints or broken twigs pointed showing them the way to go. Not even a snagged thread to clue them in on the way Eddy had taken Mia.

"We should talk to Cruz and Lincoln," Tucker said. "See

if they found anything else at Bobby and Missy's. Maybe it will point us in the right direction."

Tucker's plan was logical, but Chet couldn't just stand around and wait. Not when every second that passed was a second closer to Mia losing her life because he couldn't keep her safe.

The crunch of gravel hit his ears, and Chet turned as Cruz drove into the lot and parked, Lincoln in the passenger's seat.

The surprise of their arrival had him sprinting to the vehicle, needing to know what news the two officers brought with them.

Cruz stepped out of the car, a wide-brimmed hat blocking the rain from his face. "Find anything?"

Chet shook his head. "No trail back here, and any tracks through the thicket were washed out by this damn weather."

Lincoln joined them at the hood of the police cruiser. "Does he own any other vehicles?"

Chet rubbed the back of his neck, the skin of his cold hand colliding with the heat of his anger. "None that I'm aware of, but he couldn't get a truck back there. Hell, not even one of those compact cars could make it through these woods."

"What about a dirt bike or four-wheeler?" Tucker asked. "Something easier to get through the thicket?"

Chet stared through the trees as if he examined them hard enough, he could see exactly where Eddy had taken Mia. "Could work. But I don't see tire tracks."

"Then we press deeper into the forest. If Eddy wanted to be prepared without anyone realizing what he was up to, he could have parked something where no one would notice. Something he could get to quickly." Lincoln ducked back into the car and reappeared with a similar hat as Cruz and shrugged into a canvas jacket.

"Any chance he'd double back and bring Mia somewhere close so he can grab his truck?" Tucker asked.

"Until we know where he took her, anything's possible," Cruz said. "But I've got an officer keeping an eye on the store and his vehicle, plus someone camped out at his place, another at Bobby's, and state patrolmen are keeping an eye out as well. All the bases are covered."

Appreciation squeezed Chet's chest. The last time the woman he loved was missing, he'd felt adrift. Lost in a sea of suspicion and confusion and fear. Now, with his friends by his side, acting fast to find Mia, a beat of hope pulsed through the constant terror gripping his entire being.

"Any idea what's out there?" Lincoln asked. "I still don't know the area too well. Is there a place back in the woods he could take her? A path that leads somewhere Eddy would use? A place he'd gone hunting with his uncle as a teen? The pictures we found meant something for him to hide them for this long."

Chet searched his memories for any place that would make sense, but he didn't have a ton of memories with Eddy. He spent all his time with Tucker, with Eddy tagging along whenever he was in town. When he was lucky, Laurie would hang with them, too. But no place held a special meaning for him and Eddy. "Did you bring those pictures with you?"

Cruz nodded.

"Let me see them," he said, holding out his palm.

Cruz plucked them from the inside of his jacket and handed them over.

Chet hunched over the photos, not wanting to get them wet. The first one was of Laurie. She still had the look of innocence, with eyes bright and alive and a smattering of freckles over the bridge of her nose. His heart lurched. This is what Riley would have looked like if she'd been given the chance.

Before his emotions spilled over the surface, he flipped to the second photo. The picture of him, Tucker, and Eddy. He couldn't hide his smile. He towered over both his pals, but his limbs were long and lanky. His mouth was too big for his face and a few whiskers poked through his chin. All three of them held a large walking stick in their hands, holding them high for whoever captured the picture to see.

Tucker glanced over his shoulder and chuckled. "Damn. I haven't thought about that place in a long time."

"The fort," Chet said with a small laugh. "We were so damn proud of ourselves, even though I'm surprised it stayed up. Bobby always let us have free rein of his property. Wait a minute." He took a step away from the cluster of men and studied the patch of land in front of him once more. "This leads up the mountain then wraps around toward the cabin. Do you think that old fort is still standing?"

Tucker clapped a hand down on Chet's shoulder. "Only one way to find out."

"Everyone drive up to my place. We can walk to the fort from there."

And if they were right, and he found Eddy at their old hang out with Mia, he'd make him pay.

Mia's head fell forward, her chin pressed against her chest, when Eddy finally released her hair. Her scalp screamed, and she pressed her fingers to the back of her head to ease the pain.

"We should go inside and say hello to dear ol' Uncle

Bobby. Don't ya think?" Eddy gripped her elbow and forced her to her feet.

As she shuffled forward, she kept a close eye on the gun hanging loosely in Eddy's other hand. Either he'd forgotten he needed it to force her to stay in line, or he didn't think she posed a threat anymore and didn't have to be as vigilant.

She'd prove him wrong. She refused to be another one of his victims. She had too much to lose. Too much to live for. And even though she could run and leave Bobby alone to deal with his deranged nephew, there were now two of them to fight off one monster.

The rotting door squeaked open, and she stepped inside. Thank God she was so short or else she would have had to stoop over so her head wouldn't hit the roof. Drips of water found their ways through holes and splashed down on the dirty floor. A pile of blankets took up one corner and a wooden bench was shoved against the far wall.

The mound of blankets shifted, another wet cough breaking through the constant patter of rain beating on the roof. Bobby's gaunt face appeared as the drab, olive green blanket fell to his shoulders. Dirt smeared over his face and made the whites of his eyes more pronounced when he widened them. "Mia?"

Her name came out as if the sound itself scratched his throat. She lunged toward him, but Eddy kept her firmly in place. She ignored the sharp pinch on her bicep. "Are you okay?"

Bobby nodded, but the motion was anything but convincing.

"The old man's fine. He's been fed. Has water. I even gave him a damn blanket." Eddy tugged her to the opposite side of the room.

She kept her eyes latched on Bobby. Urgency sweeping

through her, she inched her fingers closer to her purse. Bobby was in no shape to fight. If they were going to make it out of here alive, it was up to her.

Eddy threw her in the corner, and she made a show of tripping over her feet and curling into a ball on the ground —her chest facing the floor and head against the wall. She dipped her hand into her purse and said a silent prayer of thanks she wasn't one of those women who carried around everything they owned. She made quick work of finding the knife and slid it out of the purse.

"Hey! What the hell are you doing?"

Panic made her pulse gallop. If he found the knife, she was screwed. Quickly, she dropped the weapon on the floor and turned to sit on it, then plunged her hand back into her purse. "I....I was just..."

"You think I wouldn't notice you trying to get out your phone?" He stormed to her side and yanked the purse strap over her head, throwing it across the room. "Don't be stupid, or I swear I'll drag this out. Make you watch him suffer before I finish you off."

"Leave her out of this. She's done nothing to you," Bobby yelled.

A growl of anger ripped from Eddy's mouth. He crossed the room in four long strides and struck Bobby across the mouth with the back of his hand. "Keep your mouth shut."

Mia flinched, taking the moment of distraction to grab the knife from under her, and flip open the blade. Huddling in the corner, she crossed her arms over her chest and buried her hands near her armpits. Making sure to keep the knife out of sight.

Bobby stared defiantly back, but his bound hands and ankles kept him in place on the floor.

Just like Eddy had done to Chet.

Her wrists itched. No doubt he'd do the same to her. She had to act before he fetched the rope.

"Now that she's here, I don't need you anymore," Eddy said as he stared down at Bobby. He brought his foot back and shot it forward, kicking Bobby in the stomach.

"Stop!" Mia yelled.

Eddy spun toward her, hatred shining from his eyes. "You're in no position to tell me what to do. Time's running out. I need to get this done." As if suddenly remembering the gun in his hand, he aimed it at her head. "Don't try anything stupid, or I'll make him pay." He swung the gun to Bobby.

She molded herself against the wall. As much as she didn't want him to harm Bobby, she needed Eddy's attention trained on him so she could act.

"In order to make this work," Eddy continued. "I need to make Uncle Bobby's death look like a suicide. Everyone's been lookin' for him. Knows he's been hunting."

Adrenaline coursed through Mia's veins. She couldn't just sit and watch Bobby get shot. If she could make Eddy doubt his plan, it could buy them some time. "But Chet knows you took me."

Eddy pressed the end of his gun to Bobby's temple. "No. Chet knows you're gone and *thinks* I took you. But when he finds you and Bobby dead, sees that Bobby killed himself and left an apology note, I'll show up bruised and battered. Claim I tried to stop him. Tried to save you. He'll be so destroyed by losing you—knowing his good pal Bobby was to blame—he won't stop to guess any of it."

Bobby puffed out his chest and met Eddy's stare head on. "You won't get away with this. It's too late. You need to do the right thing. I know you want to. I know you're a good boy. You don't really want to do this."

Eddy faced him, his back now to Mia. Gun still trained on Bobby. "You don't know shit, old man."

Biting into her bottom lip, Mia steeled her nerves and slowly rose to her feet. The ancient floorboards creaked with every movement. Bobby needed to keep Eddy engaged if she had a chance of sneaking up on him.

"I know I love you and you love me," Bobby said, picking up the conversation as though he understood exactly what Mia needed him to do. "I know you've had some hard times in life that weren't your fault. We can get you the help you need. I'll stand by you, son."

"Don't call me that." Eddy spat the words with so much venom she was surprised steam didn't spew from his mouth.

Creeping forward, she made herself as small and stealthy as possible. She pressed her mouth into a firm line to stop her teeth from chattering. Sweat coated her palms. She swiped her thumb over the engraved initials on the knife, feeling Chet's presence with her—giving her strength.

"Time to say goodbye. Don't worry. I'll take care of Aunt Missy."

Mia lunged forward and plunged the knife into the side of Eddy's neck then yanked it back out.

A piercing scream tore from Eddy's mouth, and he dropped to his knees, clutching the gun to his chest before falling forward. Blood poured from the wound and stained his shirt, dripping to the floor. He scrambled to his knees, trying to climb to his feet before falling forward again.

Tremors shook Mia's body as she hurried to Bobby's side then sliced the knife through the ropes around his ankles. She helped him to his feet. "Can you run?" She asked, her shaking breath coming out ragged and heavy.

"Don't worry about me. Go!"

"We should get the gun," she said, scanning the ground.

Bobby ran toward the door then stopped to stare at her. "Don't waste time girl. Let's go."

He was right. She needed to get out of there. Her cabin wasn't far. Maybe Eddy had left the keys in the four-wheeler. It couldn't be too hard to drive. Adrenaline shot through her, clawing her from the inside out and urging her to move. The rain hit her face as she stepped outside, the fire still dancing in the pit under the tarp. Her heart thudded against her chest.

The sound of labored breathing caught her ears, and she pivoted back toward the fort.

Eddy stood with the gun pointed at her. "Now you've pissed me off. I'll shred you to pieces before I kill you. Make you beg to end your pathetic little life." The pale skin of his face had gone two shades lighter. He staggered from one foot to the other, as though the slightest breeze could knock him to the ground. He had one hand pressed against the flow of blood on his neck.

But he had the gun. She had nowhere to run. Nowhere to hide.

"You sonofabitch!" Bobby screamed, running full force at Eddy with his still-bound hands raised high in the air. The poker she'd spied earlier by the fire pit in his grip.

Eddy turned to face him just as Bobby brought down the circular end of the branding stick on Eddy's cheek.

Eddy's scream of pain made her stomach roll and the hairs on the back of her neck stand tall. He reared back, aimed the gun at Bobby, and got off one shot before he fell to the ground, the gun dropping at his feet. The sound piercing the sky and splitting her eardrums.

Bobby's flesh erupted with blood and he fell to his knees. He cursed, alarm and panic widening his eyes. He pressed a hand to his side then collapsed on the ground.

Indecision slowed her mind, halting her movements. She couldn't just leave Bobby here to bleed to death alone, but lingering could be the end of both of them.

Eddy groaned and crawled toward the weapon that had dropped from his hands. His fingers wrapped around the handle.

Bobby covered his chest with his hand, blood covering his skin, and yelled, "Mia! Run!"

24

T he feel of the gun in his hand calmed Chet's nerves a fraction. He hadn't had much use of a weapon since he'd left the force, and the familiar curve of the handle nestled against his palm shifted something inside him.

Something he hadn't realized he missed.

Wrigley's fierce bark penetrated the glass of Mia's front window. He jumped up and down, wanting to be part of the group, but Chet couldn't risk springing him loose. Not when he needed to focus on finding the fort and getting to Mia, not making sure her damn dog didn't wander away and get lost.

"How far is the fort?" Cruz asked, slamming his car door and jogging to Chet's side.

Chet tucked the gun into its holster and surveyed the land. "Not far. No more than a mile. We need to go on foot. I don't want to alert him to our presence. Let him think we're still in town, chasing our tails and wondering where they are."

"We might be chasing our tails," Lincoln said. "I like our odds—this location makes sense for multiple reasons. But we need to be prepared to find this place empty."

Bang!

A distant gunshot rattled the sky and sent Chet's heart up his throat. "What do you think about our odds now?" A bite of sarcasm dripped from his words.

Otto, who lingered at Tucker's side, stood tall, nose pointed in the direction the gun had fired, then howled before taking off toward the back of the cabin.

Chet gave chase. He trusted Otto's training and his ability to find his man. The fat drops of water slowed to a dull sprinkle. Mud splashed up from the ground with each footfall and splattered his pants. He sprinted forward, his lungs burning and dots of sweat mixing with the spray of water still spitting from the sky.

The muscles in his legs screamed as he struggled to keep up with Otto, but he fixed the dog in his sightline. The cleared piece of land transformed, and he pushed into the thicket. He shielded his face with his forearm, the branches reaching out as if to grab hold of him and throw him out of the dense forest. The sound of twigs snapping behind him told him everyone else was close behind, but he didn't slow to spare them a glance.

Otto stopped short and lifted his head to sniff the air then turned and shot off again. Chet pursued him, keeping his eyes peeled for any movement. As he crept deeper into the woods, the terrain became more and more familiar. Memories assaulted him as camping trips and picnics with his friends, then later Laurie, crept into his mind.

The smell of a campfire reached his nose and he slowed. He glanced up, but the cluster of trees made it impossible to see smoke curling into the sky.

"We're getting closer," Tucker said, jogging to his side. "Otto's circling, the smoke is strong. Hard to believe Eddy could keep a fire going out here in this rain."

"Or why he'd want to," Cruz said, as he and Lincoln joined them. "If he grabbed Mia from the store on impulse, why the need to keep a fire lit in the woods during a rainstorm?"

"We'll find out soon. How much longer?" Lincoln sucked in large gulps of air as he caught his breath.

Chet dipped his chin forward, indicating the direction they needed to go. "Not too far. We should split up. Each approach at a different angle."

"Agreed. Otto and I will come in from behind." Tucker snapped his fingers and Otto trotted back to him.

"Chet, you approach from the front. Lincoln and I will come in from the sides. Be quick. Be quiet. Be careful. We don't want to spook him into doing something even more stupid." Cruz made eye contact with each of them as if to make his point clear.

Chet nodded then pressed forward, his ears tuned to anything that could point him to Mia. Wet moss covered the rough bark all around him, and his feet squished down on fallen leaves and weeds. He stepped slowly as the over-whelming ashy smell of burning logs.

A spark of light caught his attention, and he stared through the thick foliage. A fire pit encased with stones, smoke billowing then trapped under a green tarp, sat in front of the age-warped little fort covered in moss and dirt he'd built with his own two hands and the help of his friends. His pulse beat against his veins, faster with every step he took. He darted his gaze around him, unable to spot the other men, but also not spying Mia or Eddy.

A body sprawled face-down on the dirt caught his eye

and he charged forward. Terror squeezed his lungs, taking all the breath from his body.

Bobby.

Blood pooled out from his motionless body. Chet placed two fingers along the vein of his neck and found a thready pulse. Relief poured through him. Bobby was alive, but barely.

And where was Mia?

The crunch of dead leaves and debris rang in his ears, and he spun around.

Tucker and Otto bounded through the trees.

"Bobby needs an ambulance. Now." He gingerly ran his fingers along the crimson-stained shirt, not wanting to hurt him but needing to find the wound in case there was something he could do. "Gunshot wound," he yelled out.

He rose to his feet and swallowed the lump of fear clogged in his throat. His hands shook, and he racked his brain for another location where Eddy could have taken Mia. He couldn't be far. Not by the looks of Bobby.

Tucker ran forward, pulling his phone from his pocket. "I'll make the call. Look around for signs of Eddy and Mia."

A figure approached from the corner of his eye, and Chet spun to face Eddy. A gruesome wound was burned on his cheek—the brand. The skin angry and red, puss oozing from the open skin. Blood soaked through the side of his shirt.

And a gun pointed at Chet.

"It's time to end this once and for all," Eddy said, his voice weak and shaky.

Tucker hovered near Bobby and trained his weapon at Eddy. "Don't even think about. I'll rip a bullet through you so fast you won't see it coming."

"You think I care?" Eddy shouted, his gun bouncing in his hands with each angry word. "As long as he goes down with me."

Chet lifted his palms, the gun tucked along the curve of his back tickling his spine. "Where is she? What did you do with Mia?"

A feral growl combined with an evil laugh that twisted the lines of Eddy's face. "What did *I* do to *her*? Little bitch stabbed me, then the old man did this." He pointed at his face then spit on the ground. "You better find her before I do, because if I get my hands on her, I'll make her pay just like I made Bobby pay."

"Don't hurt him." Mia's frantic plea drifted through the wind, and she stepped out from behind a giant evergreen. Rain had soaked through her clothes and long strands of messy hair were plastered against her face. She spared Chet one quick glance before focusing on Eddy. "I'm the one you wanted. Leave Chet alone."

Panic beat against him like a boxer's knock-out punch to the jaw. He wanted to tell her backup was nearby and to run. To get as far away from Eddy and his gun as possible. The last thing he wanted was for Mia to sacrifice herself for him. He'd never live through the pain of losing her.

Keeping his palms high and eyes on Eddy, he inched his way toward her. "She's not a part of this, man. Leave her alone." He hated the quiver of fear that laced his words.

Smirking, Eddy tilted his head to the side. "As much as I want to make her pay, I want to see you suffer more. Everyone who was supposed to love me, loved you more. You always had everything. But now, you'll lose her just like you lost Laurie."

Moving on impulse, Chet sprinted toward Mia. Mere

220   DANIELLE HAAS

feet separated them, but it seemed like so much more. The sound of leaves shuffling reached his ears, but he couldn't stop to see where it came from. He had to get to Mia.

"No!" Tucker yelled.

When Mia was a stone's throw away, he threw himself at her as the sound of a bullet tearing from a gun hit his ears.

A scream tore through the wood, and Mia's wide, terrified eyes latched onto his.

Time slowed. Pain erupted on his torso. He gritted his teeth, ignoring the blistering as his body collided with hers and sent them both to the cold, muddy earth, the impact rattling his teeth. Not wanting to crush her, he shifted his weight as pain shot up his side.

Another gunshot rang out followed by running footsteps.

Mia laid still beneath him. Her breaths came out in short, ragged pants. Her hands trembling, tears coursing over her cheeks. "You're fine. You're going to be fine. It's all over now. Can you move?"

He rolled to his side, grimacing as his pain intensified.

"Help! Chet needs help! Now!" She scrambled to a sitting position and frantically roamed her hands over his chest and sides. "What can I do? How can I help? God, there's so much blood. I have to stop the bleeding." Her voice caught on a sob.

He rested his hand on top of hers to calm her. Shock and fear dilated her pupils. There was nothing she could do for him now. He just wanted to see her. To feel her. "Mia," he said, her name coming out on a wispy breath of air.

Tears fell onto his cheeks. "I'm right here. I'm not going anywhere."

His heart was heavy yet ready to burst. He coughed and

the motion sent spikes of pain tearing through him. "I love you, Mia. Don't ever forget that."

Unable to keep his eyes open a second longer, he drifted into darkness, Mia's sweet face the last thing he saw before he fell into oblivion.

No AMOUNT of warm air or dry clothes could stop the shivers shaking Mia from the inside out. The soft chair in the emergency waiting room did nothing to soothe her, and Brooke's firm grip on her hand was the only thing that kept her from flying to her feet and demanding to be let into the room where Chet fought for his life.

Her entire body had gone numb the second the bullet had ripped into him, and only terror had crept back since Cruz and Lincoln had charged from the woods—paramedics quickly following. But the terrifying journey to the ambulance through the woods had ended with both Chet and Bobby still unconscious. Eddy dead. And her panicked she'd never get a chance to tell Chet how much he meant to her.

Tucker sat with his forearms on his knees and hands clasped together. His still-wet clothes clung to his frame. "He's strong. He's going to pull through this." He spoke to himself as much as to the rest of them waiting to hear the outcome of both Chet and Bobby's surgeries.

Brooke squeezed her hand. "How are you holding up?"

Unable to give voice to everything swirling inside her, Mia shrugged. She'd never unsee the moment Chet flew at her, fear clear in his wide eyes.

On her other side, Zoe patted her arm. "We've got you."

Although Mia didn't doubt the sentiment, it wasn't what

she wanted. She didn't need her friends lifting her up, she needed Chet.

Lincoln and Cruz huddled together with a couple other officers, likely discussing details of the horrible scene that unfolded in the woods.

A scene that would haunt her for the rest of her days.

A doctor pushed through a set of double doors that led into the heart of the hospital and made a beeline for the cluster of officers.

Cruz held up a hand, as if to stop the doctor from speaking, and waved Mia over.

Mia shot to her feet, her legs shaky, and moved toward them. She held her breath until her chest ached.

The doctor slid a dark blue cap off his head, exposing a full head of white hair. "Mr. Black is out of surgery and in recovery."

Relief sucked the air from her lungs, and she staggered to the side.

Brooke and Zoe flanked her, holding her up and keeping her steady.

Tears dotted her eyes and she dashed them away with the tips of her fingers. "Can I see him?"

The doctor smiled. "Follow me."

Her damp shoes shuffled down the long hallway. Nurses bustled about and doctors barked out orders. They reached a room with the lights dimmed inside and the door wide open.

"Go on in. He's just waking from surgery. Keep him calm. One visitor at a time."

She shook the doctor's hand then disappeared inside. Machines dominated the side of the bed, beeping and announcing Chet's condition to people who actually understood what it meant. Chet laid on his back with a white blanket tucked around him. His eyes were closed, his body still.

She walked quietly to his side. The pale skin of his face spoke of the trauma his body had endured. Needing to feel his warmth, she rested a hand on his.

His eyes flickered open. "Mia?"

She gasped, the sound of her name on his lips the most beautiful thing she'd ever heard. "I'm here."

His fingers twitched beneath hers as if it took too much energy to do anything more. He turned his head on the thin pillow, facing her. "I'm sorry."

She furrowed her brow. "For what?"

"For letting him take you," he said, licking his dry lips. "I should have seen it. I should have known. Should have known it was Eddy."

"You need to stop blaming yourself for any part of the madness Eddy brought into our lives. None of it was your fault. And if you wouldn't have followed us—wouldn't have found me..." she shuddered, unable to put into words the horror of what could have been.

"I found you, but you stepped out of the trees to protect me. You put your life on the line—for me. In that moment, I had to do whatever I could to save you. You have too much ahead of you, too much to live for."

Tears rolled down her cheeks and his selflessness touched a part of her no man ever had. "*We* have too much ahead of us. Together. I love you, Chet. More than I ever thought possible."

All signs of pain left his face and he smiled. "I love you, too. Can I kiss you?"

She grinned and brought her face inches above his. "I thought I told you that you can kiss me senseless any time you want." Sealing her mouth to his, joy exploded inside her.

The future may be unclear, but with Chet by her side, all her dreams had already come true. He'd brought love and respect and confidence into her world. Now they'd finally put their painful pasts behind them and look forward to a brighter, better future filled with love and healing together.

EPILOGUE

C het swiped his finger over the wide, glossy screen of his new phone and muttered to himself. Why did he need to have so much crap on his phone when all he wanted was to make a call? Hell, screw all the apps Mia had made him download, he couldn't even figure out how to unlock the damn thing. Luckily, he didn't need to unlock the screen to see the time.

He shoved the cursed device back in the front pocket of his jeans. Now wasn't the time to fiddle with it. Not when Mia was due to arrive any second. Her friends and family had gathered and waited. Nerves danced in Chet's gut. He'd put this whole shindig together, wanting Mia to see with her own eyes how much support she had in Pine Valley—how large her family had grown since her time there.

Turning to the crowd of people inside the empty restaurant Mia had purchased on the town square, he pressed his finger to his lips. "Quiet. She should be here soon." Brown paper still covered the windows, but if Brooke and Zoe got Mia here on time, everyone needed to stop talking if they were going to pull off the surprise.

Hushed whispers and giggles sounded around him, but instead of irritation tightening his muscles, he shook his head and smiled. Four months had passed since the tragedy in the forest that had forced his eyes wide open about his feelings for Mia. Since then, she and Wrigley had moved to his side of the duplex, leaving her side empty for privacy, and he vowed every single day to show her how amazing she was.

In return, she'd awakened his soul and showered him with love—while bringing parts of his past into their daily lives. She'd hung pictures of his family in their home and asked questions to keep their memory alive. He could never show her how much that meant to him—but he'd damn well try.

Shadows fell across the papered-windows and anticipation had Chet bouncing on his toes. "Here she comes," he said over his shoulder.

The door creaked open, a sliver of late-afternoon light sweeping across the concrete floor. "I don't understand why you want to see the restaurant again," Mia said, her cheerful voice lifting Chet's lips. "We were just here the other day. Nothing's changed since we closed except now I have to pay the mortgage. Renovations won't start for another couple of days."

Brooke entered the room then shoved the door the rest of the way open.

"Surprise!" A chorus of voices shouted.

Mia stood in the doorway, her hands pressed against her open mouth. "What is all this?"

Zoe entered behind her and flipped on the lights. She grinned and wrapped her arm over Mia's shoulder. "Congratulations, honey. We're so happy for you."

"We sure are," Brooke said. "As long as we still get a

guest appearance from you at the retreat from time to time."

Chet stepped forward, away from the crowd of friends, and swept Mia into his arms. "I don't think you'll be able to keep her away. She doesn't know how to relax." He pressed a kiss on her cheek. "Surprise, babe."

She beamed up at him. "Did you do all this?" She extended a hand to indicate the cluster of people waiting to speak to her, as well as the tables of food that made the room smell like home.

He shrugged. "Didn't do much."

Wade laughed and approached with a drink in his hand. "Lazy guy didn't even do much of the cookin'. Somehow managed to convince me to make my chicken." He winked. "But anything for you, darlin'. Call with any questions."

Chet tightened his hold on her and scowled. No matter how secure he was in his relationship, he'd never enjoy Wade's flirting.

Mia's chuckle turned into a gasp, and she clutched Chet's sleeve. "Is that Bobby?"

"Yep. Tucker brought him and Missy. He's been getting around a little better. Don't know if he'll ever be the same, but he's a tough son of a gun." He leaned over and pointed out another guest. "Your mom's here, too."

Her eyes rounded, and she turned into his embrace, wrapping her arms around his waist. She lifted herself onto her tiptoes and pressed her mouth to his.

It took every ounce of self-control not to drag her off and deepen the kiss.

She broke away, tears swimming in her eyes. "I can't believe you did all this for me."

He lowered his forehead to hers and breathed her in. "I'd do anything for you. Surprised?"

"You have no idea. But all this—" she waved a hand

through the air. "Not the biggest surprise I've had."

A pinch of disappointment made him dip his brows low. "Oh really? And what is?"

She grinned. "You are. Never would I have imaged the grumpy, pain in my ass neighbor would end up my best friend. My biggest supporter." Her grin fell, and she stared deep in his eyes. "The love of my life."

The side of his mouth ticked up and his heart swelled. "I might have some more surprises in store for you, my love."

She hooked up one eyebrow. "You do? What?"

"You'll just have to stick around to find out." He crushed his mouth on hers, this time not caring about who watched. She was the woman he loved more than life itself, and if he couldn't shout it from the rooftops, then he'd kiss the hell out of her in front of everyone in town.

He was done hiding in the shadows, licking his wounds and keeping everyone at arm's length. He hadn't survived to sit back and watch others live their dreams. He had his own dreams to see through. Because he'd walked alone through hell and came back with the greatest victory of all.

He had Mia, and he'd love the hell out of her every damn day for the rest of his life.

～

READ about Tucker and Elizabeth in Crossroads of Obsession. They've spent years healing from the pain of the past only for the present to bring them back together....and throw a dangerous criminal in their path.

ACKNOWLEDGMENTS

I want to give a huge thank you to everyone who helped and supported me as I got Crossroads of Redemption written and out in the world. As always, the biggest thanks goes to my family. My husband, Scott, for always encouraging me, and my kids for cheering me on.

To my critique partners, Samantha Wilde and Julie Anne Lindsey, you turn my thoughts into shiny words that makes sense and let me vent on days my head is spinning. Thank you for your insight and your friendship. To Haas' Hustlers, you all rock! I can't express how much I appreciate each and every one of you!! To Kate Scholl, my trusted editor, your insight is priceless. And thank you Melinda Crown for finding my typos.

Last but never least, thank you to my readers for taking this journey with me! I love you all!
Danielle M. Haas

ABOUT THE AUTHOR

Danielle grew up with a love of reading, partly due to her namesake—Danielle Steele. It seemed as though she was born to write out the same love stories she devoured while growing up.

She attended Bowling Green State University with a dream of studying creative writing, but the thought of sharing her work in front of a group of strangers was enough to make her change her major to Political Science.

After college she moved across the state of Ohio with her soon-to-be husband. Once they married and had babies, she decided to stay home and raise her children. Some days her sanity slipped further across the line to crazy town so she decided to brush off her rusty writing chops and see what happened.

Danielle now spends her days running kids around, playing with her beloved dog, and typing as fast as she can to get the stories in her head written down. She loves to write contemporary romance with relatable characters that make her readers' hearts happy, as well as fast-paced romantic suspense that leaves them on the edge of their seats. Her story ideas are as varied and unpredictable as her everyday life.

ALSO BY DANIELLE HAAS

Injured Pride Series

Crossroads of Revival - A Prequel Novella

Crossroads of Revenge

Crossroads of Delusion

Murders of Convenience

Matched with Murder

Booked to Kill

Driven to Kill

The Sheffield Series

Second Time Around

A Place In This World

Coming Home

Stand Alones

Bound by Danger

Girl Long Gone

www.ingramcontent.com/pod-product-compliance
Lightning Source LLC
Chambersburg PA
CBHW022042240626
47154CB00007B/2525